"*Katherine, look at*

The tears fell and streamed down her face. "In your father's eyes, I will always be a servant. Think about how your family has treated servants in the past. We were possessions, cattle. We were not people with our own thoughts and desires. You're a part of that. You've treated your servants like that too—even me."

"You were never. . ." He let his words trail off. She was right. He had treated her like a servant. He had ordered her about the way he did all the others. Until he fell in love with her. "I can't accept that it's not possible for us to marry, Katherine. I admit there will be hardship at times, but God is the Lord of our lives. He'll help us."

"Perhaps. But Hiram Greene will always stand in the way," she said with a boldness he'd never heard from her.

Shelton's heart pounded. How could this be, after all this time of being patient, gently coaxing her like a skittish mare? "I love you, Katherine. Nothing should stand in opposition to that. Except God. And I believe He brought us together."

"I'm sorry, Shelton. I just can't."

He wanted to argue, but what would that accomplish? Instead, he gave her a passionate kiss. "If you ever change your mind, you know how to find me." With all the strength he could muster, he left.

God, he prayed as he climbed up on Kehoe, *move in Katherine's heart. There's nothing more I can do.*

LYNN A. COLEMAN lives in North Central Florida with her pastor husband of thirty-two years. She has three grown children and eight grandchildren. She enjoys writing for the Lord. She is the co-founder and founding president of American Christian Fiction Writers, Inc. Currently she is the E-Region Director of the Florida Writers Association. Lynn enjoys hearing from her readers. Visit her Web page at: www.lynncoleman.com

Books by Lynn A. Coleman

HEARTSONG PRESENTS

HP314—Sea Escape
HP396—A Time to Embrace
HP425—Mustering Courage
HP443—Lizzy's Hope
HP451—Southern Treasures
HP471—One Man's Honor
HP506—Cords of Love
HP523—Raining Fire
HP574—Lambert's Pride
HP635—Hogtied

A Place of Her Own

Lynn A. Coleman

Heartsong Presents

I'd like to dedicate this book to my agent, Janet Kobobel Grant, for her faith in me and in the Lord. She's been an encourager and a challenger. These are just two of the aspects of our relationship that I appreciate so much. Thank you, Janet. May the Lord continue to bless you as you work for Him and for your authors.

A note from the Author:
I love to hear from my readers! You may correspond with me by writing:

Lynn Coleman
Author Relations
PO Box 721
Uhrichsville, OH 44683

ISBN 978-1-59789-407-4

A PLACE OF HER OWN

All scripture quotations are taken from the King James Version of the Bible.

Our mission is to publish and distribute inspirational products offering exceptional value and biblical encouragement to the masses.

PRINTED IN THE U.S.A.

one

Jamestown, Kentucky, 1845

"Auntie Katherine!" The bedroom door rattled in its hinges. "Daddy says you hafta cook breakfast," her four-year-old nephew, Tucker, cried out.

Katherine O'Leary pulled the covers up over her head.

Last night, little Elizabeth Katherine, her newborn niece, had kept the whole household awake, crying. Unfortunately, it wasn't the first time. *Oh, to have solitude.* If only God would grant such a gift. *But how?*

Elizabeth's colic wasn't the only thing that had interrupted Katherine's sleep. The tragic events of the past still marred her dreams. Occasionally she'd wake from a nightmare. Prudence, her sister-in-law, and Pamela, Katherine's adoptive mother of sorts, encouraged her to not accept those thoughts, to allow God's grace to wipe them clean. And she believed He was able to do that. But the fear remained.

How could the MacKenneth family love her and her brother, Urias, as their own? Oh, it made sense with Urias, she supposed. But why her?

"Auntie Katherine!" The door rattled again.

She took in a deep breath, tossed the pillow aside, and pushed her body up to a sitting position on the edge of the bed. Urias had spared no expense in making her the four-poster bed and bedroom set. "I still wish I had my own place," she grumbled, slipping her slippers on her feet and sliding into a robe. But how could she earn the money to even buy the materials required to build her own house? Let alone actually build one.

If I were married. . . The developing knot in her stomach tightened another notch.

In the kitchen, Katherine found the morning basket of eggs, fresh from the hen house, sitting on the table. She sliced some bacon and tossed it into a large cast-iron frying pan. The tantalizing smell as it browned made her stomach wake up. She chopped a few potatoes and fried them in the bacon drippings, adding a touch of onion and some salt and pepper. After removing the potatoes, she cracked some of the eggs into the pan.

"Smells wonderful," Urias remarked as he stepped into the kitchen. Her older brother had the same red hair and green eyes she did. He pulled out a chair and sat down.

"How's Elizabeth and Prudence?" she asked, scooping the potatoes out of the frying pan and onto the breakfast plates. She placed Urias's in front of him.

"Sleeping finally. I didn't want to wake either of them. That's why I sent Tucker in to get you up. Have the boys come in from their chores yet?"

Chores were a part of farm life. Everyone pitched in from the time they could walk. "I'm assuming Vern fetched the eggs. But I haven't seen Tucker in from milking the cow yet."

Her brother put his fork down and leaned back in the chair. "You look tired. Did Elizabeth keep you up, too?"

"Yes. But it also took me a long time to get to sleep last night."

Urias narrowed his gaze. "What aren't you telling me?"

Katherine placed the hot frying pan on the counter and sat at the table, bringing a basket of biscuits with her. "I'm just tired, that's all. Been thinking foolish thoughts, like wanting my own place."

"Ah, all in good time, Katherine. You know you're welcome here for as long as you want to stay."

"I know. Thank you." How could she make him understand the deep desire for her own home? Most women went straight from living with their parents to living with a husband. Since she had no expectation of having a husband, the dream of having her own place burned within her.

"Truthfully, I considered sleeping in the barn last night." Urias chuckled.

"I hadn't thought of that." Sleeping on a bed of hay would have been better than not sleeping at all. She'd have to remember that the next time Elizabeth couldn't sleep.

Urias winked and picked up a biscuit. "Thanks for all you do."

Katherine cleaned off the remaining breakfast from the table. Did she truly want to be alone? Would she even bother to make a meal if she were by herself? She took the kettle off the stove and poured the heated water into the sink.

"Aunt Katherine!" Tucker came running, red-faced, into the room. "Vern's in the pigpen. And he's stuck."

❧

"Father, I've taken care of all your business deals as best I'm able." Shelton held a tight rein on his emotions. They'd been arguing for the better part of an hour. "I had to sell every bit of livestock just to keep a small piece of land for you and mother to have a roof over your heads. You've not only put yourself in a terrible standing with your friends, but you've ruined our family's reputation in the area. The only way the bankers would extend credit to me was if your name was no longer on the property."

Hiram Greene slumped in his chair and put his hands over his face. "I know, I know. Moving is our only option. Your mother can't live with my shame."

"Urias claims there are many business opportunities in his

area. Perhaps I'll be able to purchase some land over there. I honestly don't know. We have so little left."

"What about buying some hogs here and selling them in Virginia, like Urias did?" Hiram asked.

I'm not a farmer, like my brother-in-law, Shelton thought. *I have no idea how to herd a bunch of pigs several hundred miles.* "I have thought about that," he said. "And I might have to do it—and anything else I can to help this family."

Shelton scanned the old den. The faint smell of old leather and dried books lingered in the air. But few of the lavish furnishings remained. Everything of value had been sold to pay off debts.

"Your life won't be like it was before," he told his father. "I've managed to maintain one servant, but apart from that, you'll have to do everything around the house yourself while I'm away."

Tears welled in Hiram's eyes. "Your mother will never forgive me for what I've done."

Shelton placed his hand on his father's shoulder. "We'll get through this somehow."

Hiram nodded.

Shelton hated to see his father in this position. It just didn't seem right that a man who was so skilled in business could ruin himself gambling on a few horses. After the bank auditors went over his father's books with Shelton, it became painfully obvious that Hiram Greene had been juggling the finances for years to cover his debts. Every penny Shelton had brought into the family had gone to pay the people his father had kept at bay for so long.

If it hadn't been for the dire straights the family was facing, Shelton wouldn't leave his father alone right now. But he had two reasons for going to Jamestown, Kentucky. One was to find a place where his parents could resettle without the stigma of the loss in their social standing. The other was to find out if the love he still held in his heart for Kate was real. For years he'd been praying for her and begging God to rid him of these foolish boyhood fantasies. Instead, his attraction to her had deepened. It didn't make sense. He hadn't seen her in five years. Prudence barely mentioned her when she visited. Of course, Shelton had kept his questions to himself, not wanting to appear overly curious.

Only once had he mentioned his love for Kate, and his father had reacted vehemently. Shelton received a long and loud lecture on their family's precious standing in society, and how one couldn't lessen himself by marrying someone of a lower social class.

His father had sent him away for several months to visit with cousins. During that time Kate's brother, Urias, had found her, purchased her bond to set her free, and married Shelton's sister, Prudence.

Prudence seemed content in her simple life with Urias and the children. She had found a man who loved her for who she was and how God had knitted her together, not how society felt a woman should behave. Shelton longed for that same acceptance.

"Son," his father said, breaking into Shelton's thoughts. Hiram gazed at his son as if he could read his thoughts. "I've shamed the family enough. Don't you shame us further by getting involved with that. . .servant girl."

Shelton's back went ramrod straight. "I don't believe you have the right to speak on the matter, Father. If God works out a relationship with me and any woman, no matter what her standing in society, I would be honored to take her, if she would have me. After all, you've ruined any chance of my ever having a wife who could fit your social standard."

A deep sigh escaped his father's lips. "You're right. I'm sorry."

Shelton worried about the downcast mood his father seemed to be in lately. He acquiesced far too easily during arguments and discussions. That wasn't like him at all. But ever since Hiram's world came crashing down three months back, he'd lost all his zest for life. Even the salt wells and the businesses he'd invested in no longer held any interest for him.

"Are you certain you and Mother don't want to come with me?" Shelton asked. "Prudence must have had her third child by now."

"I wouldn't want to crowd Prudence and Urias's home, especially with a new baby. Just send a message when you've found appropriate housing and we'll come as soon as possible."

Shelton tried to ignore the "appropriate housing" reference. He wondered how his father would survive the ridicule of not being the man he had so painstakingly built himself up to be. The reality was, his father was not the man he appeared to be. His business savvy had ended years ago when he started gambling. All of his financial dealings from that point on seemed to be based on whether or not he could hedge his bets on the horses.

Shelton fought down a wave of anger. For years he'd been the only one bringing in the family income, and he never knew it. If it hadn't been for his hard work, his father's business would have gone under long ago. And his father had been less than generous in his compliments.

Shelton's only prayer these days regarded his father's humility and his own need to extend grace. Grace to a man who'd done precious little to do anything constructive for himself. Thankfully, the bank examiners saw Shelton's financial prowess long before his father acknowledged it.

For the past four years, Shelton's primary duties had revolved around the earning potential of his stud horses. He'd had to sell most of his stallions to cover his father's debts. But he still had one stud horse, plus one mare that would bring a foal in a couple of months. Between the two, he hoped he could earn enough income to keep his family fed through the winter. He didn't know what else he could do.

All he did know was that someone had to protect his mother from his father's foolishness, and he was the only son. He hoped that by going farther west his family could find a place to call home.

He'd heard folks talk about large herds of wild horses roaming the plains out west. Catching a few more mares would be the only way to build a breeding farm again.

Since horses represented his father's vanity and self-destruction, Shelton wondered if developing a different skill might be more advantageous. Digging a salt well had produced some income, but salt wells were little challenge. And he had an eye for horse breeding, no question. Besides, he needed to find his own way in this world. And he wanted a fresh start. The idea of moving to Jamestown, or even farther west, excited him.

"I expect to arrive in Jamestown in a couple of days," he told his father. "I've heard a man can sell anything in Creelsboro. Perhaps I can find some work there."

"Perhaps." Hiram stood and faced Shelton. "I'm sorry, son." He extended his hand.

Shelton pulled his father into an embrace. "It's going to work out. I promise."

Hiram nodded and walked away.

Shelton followed his father's slow movements. *Lord God, bring peace back to my father.*

Taking in a deep breath, Shelton stared at the far wall of the den, behind which he had squirreled away one prized family heirloom. He hated keeping it a secret from his father, but if Hiram knew about it, Shelton was certain he would give in and sell it.

He set his hat on his head and flung his leather saddlebags across his shoulder. If he wanted to get a jump on his journey, he had to leave now.

Kate's lively green eyes and head full of red curls flitted across his memory. Shelton closed his eyes, trying to hold on to the vision a little longer. *Lord, I love her, and she doesn't even know it. Show me if I'm just carrying on like a lovesick puppy or if what I feel for her is real.*

❧

A knock at the front door interrupted Katherine's dishwashing. She grabbed a towel and dried her hands as she headed toward the door. Between Elizabeth's crying all night and Vern getting his head stuck between the slats of the pigs' feeding trough, it had already been quite a day. Wondering what new catastrophe might be just around the corner, she opened the front door. "Can I help you?"

In front of her stood a rather handsome young man with broad but slight shoulders. He stood about four inches taller than her. "Kate?"

She gripped the doorknob tighter and nodded.

"You don't recognize me, do you?"

Tucker ran in from the sitting room. "Uncle Shelton!" he screamed in excitement.

"Shelton Greene?" Katherine squeaked.

His hair had darkened to a rich brown hue, like a fine walnut stain on a piece of oak. His eyes, which reflected the deep blue color of the sky just after sunset, drew her. The doorknob slipped through her fingers.

He knelt down and captured his nephew into his arms. "Tucker! How's your mommy and daddy?"

"Fine. Daddy is in the fields. Mommy is upstairs with 'Lizabeth."

A deep smile spread across his face. "You have a new sister?"

"Uh-huh."

Realizing she was keeping the man standing outside, Katherine stepped back. "Come on in. I'll get Prudence."

"Thank you. It's nice to see you again, Kate."

The rich tones of his voice sent a shiver across Katherine's belly. Shelton Greene did not look anything like the boy she'd known when she left his home. Now he was a man, and a rather handsome one at that. Not that she had the right to notice, she scolded herself.

"Uncle!" Vern sang out, running up to Shelton and vying with his brother for the newcomer's attention.

By the time Katherine reached the top of the stairs, she found Prudence already on her way down, with Elizabeth in her arms.

"Is Shelton really here?" she asked. Her eyes lit up with excitement.

"Yes, although I didn't recognize him."

Prudence looked puzzled, then smiled. "Oh, that's right. You didn't make the trip to Hazel Greene with us, so you haven't seen the changes in him. I was pretty shocked myself. He's matured into a rather distinguished young man."

Katherine blushed.

Prudence giggled. "It's all right, Katherine. Your secret is safe with me."

Secret? What secret? That I find the woman's brother attractive? The heat in her face intensified.

"Excuse me while I go find out what's brought him all this way."

Katherine stood at the top of the stairs. She wanted to know the answer to that question, too, but it was none of her concern. She slipped into her room to give the family some time to be with one another. But she couldn't get the image of the handsome visitor out of her head.

Unlike his father, Shelton had never treated her like a servant—well, except for that one day when he. . . Katherine stopped herself from recalling that memory. No one knew about that, and it was better left in the past.

two

Shelton stood by the mantle over the fireplace. An array of finely crafted, hand-carved animals decorated the thick shelf. "Who made these?"

"Grandpa Mac and my dad," Urias answered, escorting Prudence to the sofa. "Now that the children are down for their naps, we can finally talk. So, what brought you here?"

Shelton explained the family woes as he scanned the downstairs open area for Kate. After assuring himself that she could not hear their conversation, he leaned close to his brother-in-law and spoke in a lowered voice. "Urias, I discovered you paid my father three times the prescribed debt for your sister's bond."

Urias smiled. "Prudence and I know my mother would never have sold Katherine for such a high price. But it doesn't matter; I would have paid anything to get my sister out of servitude."

Prudence caressed her husband's arm. "How's Mother handling their situation?"

"Not well, I'm afraid. And Father isn't dealing with it either. I swear I could see him plotting another way to get money before I even left for Jamestown. I honestly don't know how to help them. I sold off the salt mines and almost all of the property to a coal mining company. That covered most of Father's gambling debts. The bankers will take the house if I don't come up with a viable plan to repay the remainder of the loan Father took out."

"Even if you do pay off Hiram's loan, do you think he could

keep himself from gambling again?" Urias asked.

"There's no guarantee. He admitted that he is to blame for the family's situation, but I sensed he wasn't completely repentant. With me gone, however, I suspect he and Mother will find it pretty uncomfortable living in the town where he lost everything."

"That might be good enough motivation for your father."

"I agree."

Urias nodded gravely. He had the same green eyes as Kate's, yet different in a way Shelton couldn't put his finger on. "How can I help?"

"Getting a job is my top priority at this point, one that will pay me enough to cover my own expenses and Father's."

"There might be work on some of the farms in the area. Crockett's paper mill may be hiring. You might even find some work on the docks in Creelsboro."

Prudence stood. "I'm going upstairs to write a letter to Mother. You two can go over all the details."

Shelton watched his sister's slow gait toward the stairs. "Is she all right?" he asked Urias.

"Elizabeth's birth took a bit more out of her than the boys, but she's doing well." Urias motioned for Shelton to take a seat, which he did. "Now, let's go over your options."

"As you know, my income from breeding horses has held off the creditors for the past year. I'm hoping I can earn a little with Kehoe and Kate." He and Urias both shared a love for breeding powerful horseflesh with sleek lines.

"We can let folks in the area know about your stud horse. Introducing new bloodlines into the local stock might be a benefit the farmers would want to take advantage of. But I don't see how it will solve the immediate problems your parents are facing."

Shelton rubbed the back of his neck. "If I sell the house and remaining land, there should be enough to buy something in this area."

"Do you have the authority to do that?"

"Yes. The bank wouldn't extend any more credit to my father until he relinquished title of the property over to me."

"I'll get the word out. We'll find some work for you. In the meantime, I can hire you on to do some of the chores on my farm. Mac and Pamela might be able to use your help, too, and since their place is right next door—"

"I couldn't do that." Shelton rose to his feet. "You're family."

Urias stood beside him and placed a hand on Shelton's shoulder. "We'll talk about it tomorrow. Tonight you can sleep on the sofa."

"The barn is fine."

"Nonsense. Like you said, you're family." Urias nodded. "I'll get some sheets and a blanket from Katherine. I suspect she's already put a kettle of hot water on for you to bathe from your journey."

"Thank you."

Urias gave him a hearty pat on the back. "We'll pray and see what the Lord says. You're welcome to stay as long as you need to. Tomorrow, if you like, we can set up a little room for you in the barn."

"I'd be most grateful."

Katherine scurried into the room, carrying a bundle of sheets, blankets, and what appeared to be a feather pillow. Shelton swooped up the bundle from her hands. Stunned, she stood there frozen, her vivid green eyes wide with some emotion he couldn't quite identify. Was it shock?

"I'm sorry. I didn't mean to startle you."

She lowered her head and looked at the floor.

"Kate, you're not my servant."

She scurried out of the family living area. A moment later

he heard a door close and latch. She was afraid of him! Why?

Shelton recalled the last moments he'd spent with Kate five years ago. He'd tried then to tell her how he felt. His tongue had felt like cotton. When he attempted to kiss her, she'd started to run away. He had ordered her to stay.

Dread suddenly filled him. He had been only sixteen—and a fool.

He plopped the linens on the sofa. Driven to clear the matter up, he marched toward Kate's room.

❧

A charge of lightning had coursed through Katherine's body when Shelton's fingers brushed up against hers. Behind the closed door of her room she felt safe. Her body leaned hard against the wall. Her mind flew back to five years ago, two weeks before Urias had come to rescue her.

Katherine hid her face in her hands. The shame, the fears. . . Her knees weakened. She fell into the bed and buried her face in the pillow. Tears soaked the quilt Grandma Mac had made for her when she first arrived.

A gentle tap on her door caused her to cling to the quilt.

"Kate, it's me," Shelton whispered. "Please open up. I wish to speak with you."

She couldn't face him. She couldn't allow him to ever be near her again.

Shelton gave another tap on the door. "Kate, I'm sorry. I just realized what you must have been thinking all these years about me. I never meant to hurt you."

Fresh tears poured down her cheeks.

"Forgive me, Kate. Please."

Katherine refused to speak. She couldn't even if she wanted to. A lump the size of an apple stuck in her throat. She slid off the bed, pulling the quilt with her and wrapping it around her. Sitting Indian style, she rocked back and forth as the demons of the past surfaced.

Memories of the beatings from her drunken mother switched to the peddler who had once owned her bond. He was a gambler, and she hadn't stayed with him long. She washed his clothes, fixed his meals, and thanked God daily that she was alive. She prayed her mother would rescue her. But Mother never came. Soon the ugly truth of what her mother had done to her became clear.

As Kate grew older she became the property of other men. No one knew the horror of the favors she'd had to endure.

"Oh, God, please don't let these memories come back," she cried into the quilt.

She had lost her faith and her identity when Wiley owned her. How Michael Pike ever purchased her bond from that ugly man, she didn't know, but she'd been grateful to be owned by someone who didn't beat her.

Hiram Greene purchased her a year after that. She'd lived with the Greenes since the age of fourteen. They had never abused her the way the others had. But watching Prudence, who was about the same age as she was, enjoying the normal pleasures a young girl would have, was difficult. And living in the Greene house, seeing all their wealth and luxury, made her life even harder. But Prudence Greene proved to be a true friend. The love she showed her allowed her to once again step out in faith and trust God. She'd asked God to forgive her for her anger, for her lack of faith, and for the sinful life she'd been forced to live.

But in moments like these, when her mind traveled over the darkness of the past, she found it hard to believe God had truly forgiven her. She knew it in her head. She knew it from His Holy Word. And there were moments when she knew it in her heart. But this was not one of those times.

"Kate?" Shelton called softly.

"Please," she moaned. "Just go away."

After several moments, she heard muffled footsteps fading away down the hall.

Katherine curled into a fetal position on the floor, not having the strength to climb back into her bed, and cried herself to exhaustion.

❧

During his first two weeks in Jamestown, Shelton performed many odd jobs at the various farms in the area, but still hadn't found full-time employment. Urias had helped in every way he could, including setting up a temporary room for him in the barn. But it seemed Shelton's best bet was to move to Creelsboro to try to work for one of the companies helping folks go west, or to work for Crockett's paper mill.

The tension between him and Kate had been constant. He wanted to get to know her as a woman, but she avoided him. She spoke in his presence only when others were around, and she hid in her room most of the time. One thing seemed certain: He couldn't be the right man for her when she was terrified of him. He had his answer.

He gathered his sparse belongings and began to pack his saddlebags. A move to Creelsboro would give Kate back the freedom to move around in her own house.

The barn door creaked. Shelton blinked at the sudden stream of light. Kate's silhouette paused, then she walked into the barn. After glancing over her shoulder, she closed the door behind her. She sneaked over to the farthest horse pen and pushed the hay from the wall, exposing the floorboards.

Again she paused and looked around. Shelton knew he should make a noise and let her know he was there, but he held his breath instead. What could she be doing?

Kate lifted a floorboard and pulled something out. He couldn't see from his angle what it was. Obviously she was hiding something, but what? And why?

She returned the item and secured the board and hay back in place.

He slipped out of the shadows. "Kate."

A startled yelp escaped her lips. Her eyes widened with fear.

He grabbed her arms. "I'm not going to hurt you."

She trembled from his touch.

He released his grip. "I'm sorry. I only wanted to speak with you, to apologize for the time at my father's house. I acted foolishly. I was sixteen and so in love with you I couldn't think straight. I should never have forced you to kiss me. That was wrong."

She nodded but kept her eyes averted.

"Kate, please speak to me. I'm leaving today."

Her gaze shot up to his. "Leaving?"

"Yes. I can't stay here and have you afraid all the time. It isn't right. This is your home. You should not live in fear of me."

Kate seemed to lose her footing and stumbled to the left. Instinctively, he reached out and caught her by the elbow. She stared at her feet once again.

"Please stop looking down. You're not a servant, and I don't like seeing you behave like this."

"Why?"

Indeed, why did it bother him so much? Oh, he knew in part it was because of his feelings for her in the past. But it went beyond that. A horrible injustice had happened to her. "I want to be your friend, Kate."

"Katherine," she corrected.

"Katherine," he repeated. "It suits you better."

"Kate's my bondage name." She squared her shoulders and stared straight at him.

"Then I'll try to never call you that again."

A slight smile crept up her cheek for the briefest of moments, then was gone as quickly as it had appeared. She gazed at the floor. "You shouldn't leave because of me."

"I just want us to be friends." With every ounce of willpower he could muster, Shelton held his hands at his side rather than lift her delicate chin. "I saw you put something under the floorboards."

She raised her head.

"What are you hiding? If you don't mind telling me."

"I do." She marched to the spot where she had been, opened her secret hiding place, and removed a small wooden box. "Now I'll have to put it somewhere else."

Shelton saw fire in this woman, despite her past. A fierce determination. His desire to get to know her grew. "You don't have to. I promise I won't touch it."

She eyed him for a long moment. "It's not really a secret. Urias made the box for me."

So why bury it? he wanted to ask, but refrained from doing so.

She traced some sort of carving on the top of the box with her finger. "I could keep this in my room, I suppose, but the boys get into everything."

Shelton chuckled. "That they do. I was always into something when I was a boy. Prudence squealed on me more times than I can remember."

She placed the box back under the floorboard. Then she stood and took a step closer to him, but kept herself at least eight feet away and did not make eye contact. "Why are you here?"

"Two reasons—and one of them is you," he yearned to say. "Father lost a lot of money gambling. I thought breeding horses here might provide enough income to support my folks and myself. I have to do what I can to help them."

She snatched a quick glimpse of him, but quickly averted

her gaze again. "Why? Shouldn't your father pay for what he's done?" Her voice quivered.

"Perhaps. But Mother is innocent. Even though I'm not proud of Father's gambling, I won't let my mother suffer if I can help it."

I don't know how I can provide for her, but I'm going to do it, somehow, with God's grace. He fought down his anger by picking up his horse brush and running it down Kehoe's neck.

"You always did like spending time with the horses."

The realization that she had noticed something personal about him brought a sweet pleasure that strengthened his resolve. "Kehoe is good stock and should sire quite a few champion horses if he's bred with the right mare. I can't wait until. . ." He hesitated, not wanting to reveal that he'd named his horse Kate. ". . .until my mare delivers." He leaned back on his heels. "Katherine, I—"

A blood-curdling scream came from the house.

three

Katherine raced toward the house. Shelton passed her and leapt to the top of the porch without touching the three stairs. The front door banged against the wall as he rushed inside. The blood pounded in her ears as she lifted her skirts higher to run faster.

Inside the house she found the family in the living room. Prudence pressed little Elizabeth close to her chest. Shelton had a small blanket wrapped around his right hand. On the floor stood a wild raccoon on its hind legs, clawing at Shelton.

"Get everyone out of the house," he ordered. "Go to Mac and Pamela's."

Katherine glanced at the gun rack over the fireplace mantle. The rack was empty. She sighed. Urias and Mac were out hunting for venison. Katherine scanned the room for the boys, then remembered they had gone to Grandma Mac's an hour earlier.

Shelton grabbed the fireplace broom and blocked the critter's path to Prudence. "Get out of here," he ordered through clenched teeth.

The two women slowly backed up the few paces to the open doorway, then ran toward the MacKenneths' farmhouse.

Tears streamed down Prudence's face.

"Are you all right?" Katherine asked, not slowing her pace. "Is Elizabeth okay?"

Prudence sniffled. "We're fine. Just terrified."

Katherine knew she should be frightened as well. Men

couldn't come within a couple of feet of her before fear washed over her. A crazed animal in the house should cause a far worse panic. Instead, she wanted to fight the small beast, take charge, and rid the house of the problem.

She stopped. "I'm going back. Shelton must have a rifle in the barn."

Prudence stopped and faced Katherine. "You take Elizabeth. I'll go help Shelton."

"No. Your baby needs you. I could never live with myself if something happened to you. I'm certain the animal has rabies."

"I've handled a rifle. Urias taught me to shoot."

A memory from the past floated through Katherine's mind, of a time before Urias left home, a time when they were a family. "Poppa taught me to shoot, too."

Prudence took in a deep breath and released it slowly. "All right. But take careful aim. I'd like my brother to grow old and gray."

Katherine ran past the house and straight into the barn. She rummaged through Shelton's belongings and found his rifle. Lifting it, she discovered it was much heavier than the one her father had shown her so many years before. It also had two barrels. Could she shoot this and not hit Shelton? Fear slithered through her body. Her breathing became more ragged. She closed her eyes and slowly inhaled. She couldn't let fear control her now, as it had so often in her life.

She reached for the lead bullets and powder, loaded the two barrels, and marched toward the house. The sheer weight of the gun forced her to carry it with both hands. How could she possibly fire it?

The angry growls of the sick creature cut through the air.

Katherine quickened her pace and lifted the rifle as she crossed the open threshold.

Shelton pivoted around to see who had entered the house. The wild animal lashed out and bit him on the leg.

She aimed the rifle but did not have a clear shot of the raccoon. Shelton kicked, forcing the animal to let go, but it bit down again. He whacked the broom handle across the raccoon's head.

Dazed, the creature fell to the floor. Katherine aimed and pulled the trigger. A clean shot perforated the raccoon with lead balls.

Shelton cried out in pain and leaned against the wall.

"Take your pants off," Katherine ordered. "We must clean that wound."

❧

Shelton reached for his belt buckle but thought better of it. "Give me that knife." He pointed to the large carving knife hanging on the side of the kitchen cabinet.

Kate placed the gun on the table and hurried to the cabinet.

Shelton gritted his teeth against the excruciating pain.

"The animal looks rabid," Katherine said as she handed him the knife.

He glanced at the heap of fur and fangs. Foam dripped from the creature's jowls, leaving no doubt as to its condition. The question was, could he survive this attack? "Boil some water," he ordered.

Kate's back stiffened. He'd done it again, made her feel like a servant. "Please," he amended.

Kate nodded and did as he'd requested.

Setting the tip of the blade against the outer seam of his pants, he ripped the material from the knee down. Blood poured out of a deep wound. One of his arteries must have been punctured.

He watched Katherine fill the lower front part of the step-up cast-iron stove with kindling. He opened his mouth to tell her to add more for a quicker blaze, but promptly closed it. Kate would know her way around a stove.

Shelton didn't like seeing this side of himself. Had he always been this insensitive to others? Had he looked down on people stationed in a lower social class than his own? Was he as guilty as his father of treating Kate like a servant?

A fresh wave of pain coursed through his body. He let out an audible groan.

Katherine turned and ran toward him.

Shelton blinked. The room began to spin. He slowly closed and opened his eyes, trying to focus.

"Sit down," Kate ordered. Authority oozed from her command. He'd never seen her like this. He followed her order.

"Place your injured leg on this chair." Kate pulled his flapping pant leg away from his skin. She leaned closer to the wound. "It's deep and nasty. You might need some stitches. That coon must have twisted back and forth once he got his teeth into you."

"It felt like it."

"I'm going to get some cloths to wash the wound." She started to leave.

"Don't touch it, Katherine. I don't want you getting sick."

A slight turn of her delicate pink lips made him aware that she was pleased about his concern for her. *Perhaps there is a chance for us to develop a relationship after all.* Then again, how many days did he have left? The mortality rate from rabies didn't give a man a lot of hope. *Please, God, if we're to be together. . .* Wasn't that the real question? Were they meant to be together? Apart from this momentary act of kindness, Kate was still terrified of him.

"I'll be right back. Don't move."

He gripped the chair tighter in her absence. He couldn't let her see how much his leg hurt. The large knife lay on the table. Shelton picked it up and tried to get a good angle to lance the wound.

"What are you doing?" Katherine stood before him, her hands on her hips.

"I have to get out the poison."

"This isn't a snakebite."

"I know, but—"

"We need to wash it first."

"Katherine, are you in there?" Pamela MacKenneth called out from the porch.

"In the kitchen. Shelton's been bit."

"Ain't that bad," he lied.

Pamela flew into the room and examined his leg. Shelton felt like a lame horse lying on the ground with a gang of people looking over him trying to decide if they should shoot him and put him out of his misery.

"Pour water over the wound, Katherine. Flush it out several times. Then we'll pour hot water over it—as hot as he can take it—to try to kill off any infection before it starts."

Katherine pumped a pitcher of water and poured it over his leg.

"You're losing a lot of blood," Pamela said, washing her hands in the sink, then wiping them on a dishtowel. "We're going to have to stitch up the wound. Katherine, where does Prudence keep the whiskey?"

"Upper right-hand cupboard. I'll get a needle and thread. And some towels to clean up that mess on the floor."

"Thanks."

Shelton's eyelids drifted shut. He forced them to open. They complied only halfway. He had to fight.

Then again, why? *Heaven is a wonderful place*, his mind sluggishly told him.

Mother needs me, he inwardly debated. He forced his eyes to open farther. They slid right back down.

"He's losing a lot of blood," Kate said.

"Take off his belt and make a tourniquet."

After a moment's hesitation, Katherine unhooked his belt and pulled it off of his hips.

Pamela held a glass of golden brown liquid to his lips. "Drink this."

He sipped. It burned a path down to his stomach.

The pressure Kate applied as she wrapped the belt around his leg made him want to kick her away. He bore down on the back of the chair and groaned.

"Finish the whiskey, Shelton."

The warmth of the liquid nectar started to calm his body. *No wonder a man can get addicted to this stuff.*

The pain began to subside. His mind grew more fuzzy. A smile developed on his lips. Images of Katherine wrapped in his arms swam around in his head. "Oh, my sweet, sweet, Kate."

❧

"We can start now," Pamela said. "He's rambling about his horse."

"His horse?" *Or me?* Katherine loosened the tourniquet. Blood poured instantly from the wound. She tightened it again.

Pamela pulled the thread through the needle and began to repair the wound while Katherine held the injured leg still.

Fifteen minutes later, Pamela had sewn the last stitch and Shelton started snoring. "We're going to have to move him, and I'm afraid the only open bed is in your room. We can't have him exposed to the children."

"I understand."

"I'll help you get him to bed. Then go scrub yourself 'til you're pink. I left room between the stitches so the blood can escape as the artery bleeds. You'll need to stay the night with him, opening and closing that tourniquet every fifteen minutes. Can you do that?"

"I'll try."

Pamela nodded. "I know it'll be hard staying awake all night. Then again, I hear Elizabeth doesn't allow for much sleeping anyway."

Katherine chuckled. "True."

Together they lifted Shelton by the shoulders and dragged him onto her bed. "Keep the wound moist for a long as possible. Moisture helps the rabies bleed out of the body."

A shiver of fear slithered down Katherine's spine at the thought of spending so much time alone with a man.

"Are you all right?" Pamela asked.

"Fine. He just weighs more than he seems to."

Pamela chuckled. "Be glad he's only five-seven. Try heaving Mac into bed. Worst patient I ever had. Thankfully, he is rarely ill."

Mac MacKenneth was a huge man, but he didn't scare Katherine. Not like Shelton did. Of course, she'd only known Mac as a happily married man, a good Christian man.

"Guess I'd better go burn that raccoon," Pamela said.

"I'll clean up."

"Open the tourniquet again first. Then go clean."

Katherine nodded. *Lord, help me be a good nurse to this man, even though I am terrified of him.*

For hours, she sat by his bed, doing her best to follow Pamela's instructions and to understand her own emotions. Shelton was an attractive man. And he seemed so kind, so brave. Why did she fear him?

She noticed sweat beading all over his bronzed skin. A fever was rising.

four

Shelton ached from head to toe. His leg felt like it was on fire. Kate's gentle ministrations eased the pain somewhat. He licked his parched lips and opened his eyes. She sat curled up in a chair next to the bed. Her golden red hair cascaded over her shoulders as she slept.

He blinked and refocused. He'd never seen her with her hair down. His mind must be playing tricks on him. Kate's hair always sat on her head, with no more than a few wisps falling down the sides.

Shelton's leg ached. He reached down to release the pressure on the tourniquet, but it wasn't there. He leaned back again. The slight movement made him groan.

Kate jumped upright. "I'm sorry. I fell asleep. What's wrong?"

"Where's the tourniquet?"

"Mac came by and examined the wound, as well as his wife's handiwork. He said to take off the tourniquet. Slight bleeding will help the healing."

"Does he think. . ." Shelton knew rabies could be fatal. But he couldn't form the words in his mouth.

"Mac said only time will tell."

Shelton closed his eyes. *Father God, please keep me alive to help my family.*

Katherine placed a cool, damp cloth on his forehead. "Shelton, why did you send us away? If I had stayed. . ."

"Prudence and Elizabeth were in danger." He focused on her deep green eyes. "And so were you."

"I. . ." She clamped her mouth shut.

What was she going to say? They hadn't spent much time together since his arrival two weeks ago, but several times, he'd seen her stop herself from saying what was on her mind.

"Speak," he ordered.

She narrowed her eyes. "I am not your servant. I will not be ordered about like a. . ."

A twitch of pleasure pulled at his lips as he tried to suppress a smile.

"What?" Her nostrils flared.

"Kate. . .I mean, Katherine. . .I didn't mean—" A surge of pain raced up his leg. "Please, go back to your room. I'm fine."

Katherine stepped back and blinked. In a soft whisper, she said, "This is my room."

Shelton appraised his surroundings. The furniture was well made, hand crafted by Urias, no doubt, but it lacked the feminine look and smells he remembered of Prudence's room. He lifted the covers to slip out of bed. "I'm sorry. I'll go to the barn."

"You'll do no such thing." Katherine stomped her foot for emphasis. "You're to stay off that leg for at least two days. And I'll not be facing Pru's wrath for the rest of my life by being responsible for your death."

He leaned back against the headboard. "Katherine, you're not responsible."

"Yes, I am." Her face flushed. "If I hadn't come into the house when I did, you wouldn't have been bitten. This is all my fault."

He reached out to her.

She stepped farther into the shadows. "Go back to sleep. It's late. You need your rest."

Not wanting to move his leg again, he closed his eyes. The room darkened. The door creaked. Katherine had left him. If only he could let her slip out of his heart as easily.

❧

Katherine pulled the quilt higher over her shoulder as she shifted on the living room sofa. She hadn't gone back into her bedroom since Shelton had woken up. How could she have thought that she could spend the night in there with him and care for him?

A gentle hand shook her shoulder. "Your room is free now," Urias said. "I helped Shelton move back to the barn. And Prudence changed your sheets."

"How is he?"

"He's fine. Mac says the wound is healing well. You did a good job. Now, go to bed and get some sleep."

Katherine lifted her head from the sofa and stared through her bedroom doorway. Why had Urias taken Shelton out to the barn? Did it bother Shelton to be in her room?

"You could have left him in there."

"Shh. He's fine. Mac and I will take good care of him. You just rest."

She couldn't argue. It seemed like ages since she had a good night's sleep.

❧

Katherine woke to the smell of fresh meat roasting. How long had she been asleep? She dressed and headed into the kitchen.

Prudence looked up from basting the meat that sat in the large pan. She beamed. "Good morning, sleepy head."

"What time is it?"

"Going on near five," she said as she slid the roast back into the oven. "Dinner is just about ready."

"I slept the day away?"

"Your body seemed to require it." Prudence closed the oven door, then stood and stretched her back. "Tell me, did the old nightmares return?"

Katherine drew herself up straight. "Why do you ask?"

"You cried out during the night."

The tiny muscles around her spine seemed to tighten even more.

"You should tell Urias about the abuse you've suffered. Your brother is not a foolish man. He knows what goes on in the hearts of evil men."

"I don't want to. Besides, he's better off not knowing."

Prudence floured her hands and began to shape the biscuit dough. "The only way to rid yourself of these demons is to share them with the right person. You've told me a few things, but I know you haven't revealed all that happened to you. Perhaps your own flesh and blood. . ."

Katherine stared at the floor. "I'll think on it."

Prudence wiped her hands on a clean towel. "Promise?"

"Aye."

"I love the Irish brogue you slip into from time to time. Urias does it, too. You two are so much alike."

Katherine could not see the comparison. They were brother and sister, so they shared similar physical features, but Urias lived such a contented life. Even after opening her heart to God last year, she didn't feel much different. She still felt damaged. *A sinner will always be a sinner.* Katherine sighed. She would never be truly free from the tyrants who once owned her.

Prudence pulled her into a hug. "Remember, Katherine, you are free in Christ. You're not in bondage to past sins. Jesus has forgiven you."

"I know." *But I still feel bound to the past. What's wrong with me?* She knew she wasn't trusting in the Lord as she should.

Katherine forced a smile. "What can I do to help?"

"Finish setting the table while I put the food into the serving dishes."

As Katherine arranged the plates on the table, a deep-seated fear washed over her. Should she tell Urias about her past? Or keep her problems to herself?

Throughout the meal, Katherine kept a barrage of questions flowing toward the children. She didn't want to think about last night's nightmare. She didn't even remember having one.

After the children were put to bed, Urias joined her in the sitting room. "You should get some sleep, too, Katherine. I'm going to Creelsboro in the morning for Shelton. While I'm gone, his bandages will need tending. And Prudence could use a hand with the children."

A contorted smile rose on her lips. If she arranged things well, perhaps she could go to Creelsboro, too. It was time to start moving on with her life.

❧

Shelton leaned on the makeshift cane and hobbled about the barn. He'd been up since the crack of dawn, waiting on Urias. He knew his leg wasn't up to a horse ride, but with a little luck he might persuade Urias to take the buggy instead. They could tie Kehoe to the rear. Anyone who knew good horseflesh would spot Kehoe's qualities a mile away.

"Shelton?" Katherine whispered as she poked her head into the barn.

"Over here."

She turned toward his voice, squinting in the diffused light of the barn. "Urias said he was going into Creelsboro for you. Why?"

"He agreed to try to find some breeders there who might take a look at Kehoe. If we can catch some settlers going west, I'd offer them a discounted rate for quick cash."

She glanced behind her shoulder. Shelton guessed she didn't want anyone to see her in the barn alone with him.

"When is the season for breeding horses?"

"All year, but mainly spring till fall." He leaned hard on his cane. "I was hoping to convince Urias to take the wagon this morning and let me come along."

"Perhaps I could go with you instead. I've been meaning to take a trip to Creelsboro."

"Are you sure?" Shelton brushed her hand with his. "We'd be sitting side by side."

I'll do whatever's necessary. "I have to go into town."

"You're safe with me, Katherine," he assured her.

A single nod. No words, no eye contact. *What has happened to her?*

"You're bleeding." She pointed to his trousers. "Perhaps we'd better go another time. Right now, you should concentrate on getting well."

"I'm fine." He held the cane tighter as a wave of dizziness washed over him.

Katherine placed her hands on her hips. "You're being awfully pig-headed."

Shelton wanted to spar with her but decided not to push this new willingness to spend a little time with him. "Wait over there," he said, pointing toward the large barn door, "while I change my trousers."

She raised her right eyebrow as if to question him, then lowered it and went out the door.

He removed his boots and pants, then wrapped a blanket around his waist. "You can come in now."

Urias appeared in the doorway. "Katherine says you had a foolish idea of running into Creelsboro today."

"I thought with the wagon—"

Urias wagged his head. "You obviously weren't thinking." He scanned the bleeding wound. "Katherine will clean that up. But you're getting back in that bed."

"Urias—"

"And if you get out again before I say you're ready, I'll personally set a hundred-pound keg on your chest to hold you down." Urias glared at him until Shelton sat on the bed, then he stomped out of the barn.

Katherine entered moments later with a fresh basin of water and a clean cloth. Merriment danced in her eyes.

"You think this is funny? Your brother is ordering me about like a child."

"He is a very protective man."

Pain shot up Shelton's leg, like a knife cutting deep into his skin. He moaned.

Katherine came to his side. "Lay your head down. I'll take care of this."

He wanted to resist, but the dizziness he'd experienced earlier hadn't entirely left and he felt the room spinning. The soft pillow encircled his head. Katherine placed her delicate fingers on his forehead. "You have a high fever. You should stay down and let your body heal."

"Yeah," he mumbled. He'd lie there forever if she'd stay by his side.

She placed a cool cloth on his forehead. Then he felt her heavenly touch on his leg.

"It's still a little red, but the blood is drying to a dark brown scab. That's good. It means there be no sign of infection. You should be up and around in no time."

Shelton chuckled. "I like your Irish brogue. You don't use it much."

"No, I don't."

"Why not?"

Katherine applied some pressure on the wound. Shelton grimaced. "Sorry. I'll try to be more gentle."

"You're fine. It's just sensitive. Thank you for all your help."

She acknowledged with a simple nod of her head.

Shelton wished she would open up and confide in him. "Katherine, what's your biggest desire in life?"

"A place of my own," she blurted out. Her hand stilled. "I'm sorry, I didn't mean to say that."

Shelton sat up, adjusting the blanket to maintain modesty. "Your secrets are safe with me." He winked, remembering the day he'd discovered her secret hiding place in the barn. He'd kept his word and never looked to see what she had hidden in that small box. Perhaps it was a tidy sum of money she'd saved in the hope of being able to someday afford a place for herself.

"Why did you want to go to Creelsboro?"

"I'm hoping to find some work, as a seamstress perhaps. I'm not smart enough to be a teacher, although Grandma Mac has been giving me lessons. My mom didn't care much for book learning. But I've learned a lot since I moved here."

"I think you're a very smart woman." He could see her in a schoolhouse, teaching the children and living in a private room off the back. Unfortunately, there didn't seem to be a place for him in that picture. "Seamstress, huh?"

"Yes." She smiled.

"I may have a small job for you. Perhaps you could repair the trousers I had on the day of the raccoon attack?"

"Of course."

"I'd be happy to pay you."

"There's no charge for family."

"I'm not your family, Katherine." *But I want to be.*

"Close enough. You're my brother's brother-in-law." Katherine chuckled. "Besides, I thought you were going to Creelsboro in order to earn some money."

"I told you you're a smart woman."

She wrapped the clean linen around the wound and secured it. "All done. I'll leave you now and send Vern in with lunch later. Get some rest. You're looking pale."

"Thank you, Katherine."

He watched her leave, then took in a deep pull of air. He leaned back against the headboard of the old bed. Perhaps he still had a chance with Katherine after all.

Shelton reached over to the small table, which held a glass of water and some herbs that Mac had brought in. His head started swimming and he felt like he could fall out of bed without even moving. He'd deal with Katherine another day. Today he had to concentrate on recovering and living.

With time, he might just be able to win her heart. *But only if she gives it to me freely*, he reminded himself. He would not force her. He would not demand. He would wait patiently, treating her like a skittish mare.

That's it! He smiled and knitted his fingers together behind his head. Katherine was like a wild mare; a firm but gentle hand was in order for her to trust him.

five

Katherine pumped water into the barrel to wash clothes. Urias had built an outdoor shelter for a laundry room of sorts for spring and fall cleaning. It was the time to get all the quilts, blankets, and sheets ready for winter.

As she agitated the water, she thought back on the past couple of days and caring for Shelton. It seemed odd but good to be near a man and not be frightened. They talked more and more, and for the first time in her life she felt like she had a male friend.

On the other hand, she noticed things about him that seemed totally inappropriate. Like how handsome he was, and how strong his hands were. She wondered what it would be like to be held in his arms. She shook off the images and went back to cleaning the dirty clothes.

"Katherine?" Shelton's voice spun around her spine, giving her strength, not fear. *Thank You, Lord.* "Would you like to travel to Creelsboro with me tomorrow?"

She dropped the agitator in the barrel and dried off her hands on the long apron that protected her dress. "Do you think you're well enough?"

"I believe so. I wouldn't want to stress my leg too much, but the buggy would allow me to put it up some."

Katherine thought about the wagon. It had a panel in front, and they could both place their feet up there. "Has the fever returned?"

"No, thank the Lord. Mac says that I'll have to wait another week before we know for certain if I'm affected. But the prognosis looks good."

Katherine fired off another prayer for Shelton. She didn't want to lose her friend.

"Are you still hoping to obtain employment in town?" he asked.

A slight heat rose on her cheeks. She'd wanted to go the other day to find a job. She'd also entertained the hope of finding a man heading west who might want a wife. After a couple of days of prayer, however, she knew that wasn't the answer. If she were ever to be given the gift of a spouse, it would have to be for more than convenience or escape. Oddly, the person she'd wanted to escape from was the one she now wanted to be near.

"Katherine?"

She snapped from her musings. "Forgive me, me mind was rambling."

"If you'd rather I not know your personal dealings, I understand." Shelton leaned against the rail.

"I have some items I've sewn that I'm hoping to sell to the merchants."

"Speaking of sewing, thank you for mending my trousers."

"You're welcome." She reached for the agitator.

"Well, I'll leave you to your task. I didn't mean to interrupt."

"Shelton." She paused. She'd just about confessed to him that he wasn't an interruption. "Why did you name your horse Kehoe?"

"It's a derivative of the Irish word for horse."

"Really?"

He looked at his feet.

"Why would you choose that name, then? You're family isn't Irish, is it?"

"No." A deep crimson color ran up his neck. He cleared his throat. "It just. . .seemed like the right name at the time."

Am I the reason? Katherine dropped the wooden handle. *Lord, it doesn't make sense. I was just his servant.*

"Katherine." He reached out to her. "I've always cared a great deal for you."

She resisted the temptation to place her hand within his. Physical contact with a man, apart from tending to his wounds, was something she didn't want to venture into. A violent flash from the past cut off her vision. Instinctively she rubbed her right wrist. She squeezed her eyes shut against the pain, the horror.

"Katherine?" Shelton's voice soothed her. His hands landed ever so slightly on her shoulders.

Her heart raced. Cold sweat beaded across her forehead and upper lip, then total darkness.

❧

Shelton caught Katherine's body before her head smashed on the ground. *What's wrong with this woman? One moment she's fine, the next she faints.* Hoisting her delicate frame in his arms, he carried her to the house. "Prudence," he hollered, kicking the closed door with his foot.

His sister opened the door. "What happened?"

"I don't know. We were just talking and the vapors overtook her."

"Place her on her bed. I'll get a cool compress."

Shelton thought back on their conversation just before she passed out. He hadn't said anything upsetting to her. He'd just been embarrassed. How could he explain that he'd loved her so much he named his horse after her?

Shelton laid her across her bed. The same bed he had lain in right after the raccoon attack. He groaned.

"She's not that heavy. You must be losing your strength, little brother." Prudence placed a cool cloth on Katherine's forehead.

She moaned.

Praise You, Lord, she's all right. "Why would she just faint like that?"

"Women do that from time to time."

"Oh." The idea of it being a female issue disconcerted him so much he fumbled his way out the door and left his sister to tend to Katherine. *Thank You, God, that I was born a man!*

He heard voices and knew Prudence and Katherine were speaking. He set his hat more firmly on his head and marched outside. Every fiber of his body urged him to do something, anything. A ride, he decided. Taking Kehoe for a hard jaunt sounded wonderful.

In the barn, he saddled his horse and headed south toward Creelsboro.

Thirty minutes later, Shelton pushed Kehoe to a fast gallop. He couldn't remember the last time he'd taken the animal out for a decent run. A good workout would be healthy for Kehoe, not to mention how much it would benefit his owner.

A small stream of sweat rolled down Shelton's spine. He eased up on the reins and patted Kehoe's neck. "Feel good, boy?"

Shelton stopped at Jobbes Fork and let the horse drink. Kehoe enjoyed the speed. Shelton did, too.

The gentle run of the river soothed Shelton's rankled nerves. Perhaps Prudence was right and Katherine was just having some kind of female problem. But from the way her eyes went distant a couple of times during their conversation, he didn't think so. *She's like a timid mare, Lord. Only worse. More like a battered horse.*

"No, Lord," he prayed. Surely nothing that serious had happened to Katherine. But a few days back he'd had a similar thought.

Shelton hoisted himself off Kehoe. The leather creaked as he steadied his feet on the ground.

Did he really want to know about her past? His mind imagined the worst thing that could be done to a female child. It made his stomach churn.

Lifting a twig, he pierced the packed sand of the riverbank. He jammed the stick in farther. "I'm madder than a snake, Lord. I know I shouldn't be, but I am. Men like that should be hung." He walked along the edge of the river, reminding himself not to assume something he didn't know for sure was true.

The wind stirred the top of the pine trees across the river. Water cascaded over a fallen tree trunk. "Lord, take this anger from me. I don't like being this way."

Working at the mill was beginning to sound better all the time. It would be steady work, and the more Shelton felt anger building up in him the more he needed to do some physical exercise. Unfortunately, being a part of the higher social circles, he'd never learned to do much of anything other than take care of his horses.

With determined steps he limped back to his horse and headed toward Crockett's paper mill. It was time for him to get a job. If he was hired, he'd save all his money and buy some land. Perhaps in a year he'd have a place built for his parents. Then he could think about becoming involved with Katherine. Maybe by that time he could handle his mixed emotions.

❧

"Are you feeling better?"

Katherine smiled at Prudence, who was adjusting the cool compress against her forehead. "I'm fine. I don't know what came over me."

"When did you eat last?"

Katherine thought for a moment. At breakfast she'd nibbled at the counter, but didn't sit down to eat with the family. "I had a piece of bacon this morning."

"That's not enough," she chided. "Now, tell me what happened out back."

Leaning her head into the pillow, she closed her eyes. "A dark memory overcame me." She'd leave it at that. Prudence wouldn't pry.

"That's been happening a lot lately, hasn't it?"

Katherine nodded.

"Is it because my brother is here?"

"I thought so at first, but now I'm not sure. Maybe this will be the last time."

Prudence gave her a slight smile. "Stay in bed and rest for a while. I'll send Tucker in with something for you to eat."

"Thank you." Normally she would have objected at having someone wait on her, but today she didn't have the strength to fight. "Prudence?"

"Yes?" Her sister-in-law turned in the doorway.

"I think it's time for me to move to Creelsboro, find a place of my own. I can supply some of the merchants with articles of clothing to sell."

Prudence shook her head. "Please don't make any plans right now. If you can stay a little longer, you might not want to move to Creelsboro."

Katherine sat up on the bed. "What are you talking about?"

"I can't say right now. I'll speak to Urias and tell him your plans." Prudence turned to leave.

"Pru?"

"Talk to Urias," she said as she left.

"Where is he?" Katherine called out, but no one answered.

Urias and Mac had been gone a lot lately and they seemed to bring little home from their expeditions. That was quite unlike them. Mac could track anything, anywhere. He wasn't Indian, but he'd spent a lot of time with some before marrying Pamela.

Katherine picked up her sewing kit and the shirt she'd been making for Shelton. If she were to move out on her own, she'd have to sell it to help pay the rent.

She enjoyed the special friendship she shared with Prudence. But the desire to move away from the house was stronger now than it had ever been. Shelton was the cause of that.

No, she admitted, it wasn't Shelton's fault. Katherine closed her eyes. "Lord, it's my own sinful desires. How can I even entertain the thought of wanting to be in a man's arms after what I've been through? I can't ruin Shelton's life. I'm not fit for marriage. And he talks daily about providing for his parents. I know I could never be comfortable around Hiram Greene. Please, Lord, help me. I can't be a burden to my brother any longer."

She wiped her eyes at the gentle knock on her bedroom door.

"Auntie Katherine," Tucker called. "Mommy said to give you this."

"I'll be right there." Katherine folded the sewing and left it on the chair. She opened the door.

Her nephew stood there, a tray of food and drink balancing precariously on his little hands.

"Thank you." As she took the tray, the boy sighed with relief.

"Auntie Katherine, are you all right?"

"Yes, dear," she said, setting the tray on her nightstand. "I just didn't eat enough this morning."

"Why?" He placed his hands on his hips, imitating her.

"Because I got busy and forgot."

"That's silly. Everyone knows you have to eat."

Katherine ruffled Tucker's dark curls. "You're absolutely right."

Apparently quite pleased with his astute powers of observation, Tucker puffed up his chest and headed toward the kitchen. He was quite the charmer. Not unlike his uncle.

Katherine groaned at the thought as she bit off a hunk of her sandwich. She saw Shelton everywhere. Frightened by her growing attraction to him, she prayed she would not give in to carnality.

six

Every inch of Shelton's body ached. He'd never worked so hard in all his life. After two days at the mill, he had blisters on his blisters and several had popped. He pulled off his work gloves to see how badly his hands bled today.

He left every morning before the rest of the family stirred. The trek to the mill took an hour on Kehoe. The stallion loved the exercise. But ten hours a day of back-breaking work forced Shelton to once again wonder whether he could ever make a living suitable enough to support his parents. The idea of running a herd of hogs to Virginia for some quick cash looked better every day.

On the other hand, going west seemed promising. People came to Creelsboro from all over, heading through on their way to the frontier. Land opportunities abounded, and rumor had it that horses roamed the plains in huge herds, with plenty for the taking.

His parents would never go that far west. His father wanted to stay in Kentucky, and his mother would want to be near their grandchildren. When he gave them some.

"Get back to work, Greene," the foreman hollered over the sound of saws, hammers, and axes.

Shelton waved and put his gloves back on. Another hour of cutting logs and he'd be able to go home for the night. "Home." He snickered and rolled the next log to be split. *I'm living in a barn.*

Eight months ago he was living in a mansion and didn't have a care in the world. His food and clothing were prepared for him every day. His only concern was how to acquire and breed more horses. *Now look at me.* He'd had to sell off almost all his stock, and he had no home to call his own. *Lord, I don't know what to do.*

The sledgehammer seemed to weigh more than it did two days ago. Shelton grabbed the iron wedge and positioned it in the log. The sharp smell of freshly cut wood invigorated him. He raised the mallet and heaved it down on the wedge.

The clang of the quitting bell rang. Shelton dusted off his work clothes and peeled off his gloves.

"You ain't worked much, have ya?" Frank Smith blustered, staring at Shelton's fingers.

"Not this kind of work."

"Humph. You'd best be putting some teat salve on them hands tonight."

"Teat salve? You mean the stuff folks use on cow udders?"

"Yes, sir. Takes the bite out of them blisters like nothing else around. Check a dairy farmer's hands. They always be soft as a baby's bottom."

Shelton looked at his cracked and bleeding palms. He'd try anything at this point.

"Greene, come on over here," Mr. Crockett called.

"Thanks, Frank."

"You'd best get to Mr. Crockett right quick iffen you wants to keep this here job." Frank set a cap on his head and hiked up his collar.

Shelton ran to the main building. "What can I do for you, sir?"

He handed Shelton a brown envelope. "I'm sorry, son, but I'm afraid I have to let you go. Your work was half the amount of the others. I gave you a full day's pay. I know you tried hard."

Shelton's shoulders sank right along with his spirits. Without a word, he reached out for the envelope. Mr. Crockett didn't release it.

"You interested in selling that stallion of yours?"

"No, sir."

"It appears to me you need to earn some money quickly. Why won't you sell?"

Shelton squared his shoulders. "Kehoe is my future. I might be in short supply of capital right now, but if I were to let go of Kehoe, I'd be setting back my plans by five years."

"You a breeder?"

"Yes, sir. Kehoe is prime horse flesh."

"He's got good lines. Is he fast?"

"Yes, sir."

"Want to test his skills against my three-year-old? If your horse wins, I'll double your pay. If mine wins, you sell Kehoe to me for a fair price."

Shelton held back a laugh. Then it dawned on him how easy it would be to fall into gambling, just like his father.

"Mr. Crockett, with all due respect, that offer is hardly worth considering. I've never seen your horse, let alone know how well he runs. If I were to blindly wager my future against yours, what profit would I have? I'd consider a friendly race between men, but I will not gamble my future away."

Mr. Crockett scrutinized Shelton with the cunning of a hawk looking over his prey. "Done. A friendly race, nothing more."

"That, sir, is acceptable."

"William," Mr. Crockett yelled. "Get Bailey."

"If you don't mind, I'll be soaking my hands while we wait for your stallion."

A smirk rose from the corners of Mr. Crockett's mouth. Shelton walked to the pump, filled the bucket, and soaked his hands in the icy water.

Feeling slightly relieved, but shivering with cold, he crossed to the holding pen, where Kehoe stood munching on some hay. "How are you, boy?"

Kehoe nuzzled his nose into Shelton's chest.

"We're going to have some fun today." Shelton cinched the saddle and readied Kehoe with some prancing around the mill yard.

Mr. Crockett's three-year-old stallion trotted into the yard. He had a chestnut coat with white boots. His muscles seemed taut and ready for action.

"Wanna race him, boy?" Shelton whispered in his horse's ear.

Kehoe raised his head and pranced in place. Shelton tightened his grasp on the reins. Kehoe loved speed, and today he'd be able to use it.

❧

Katherine didn't know what to do with herself. Prudence had prepared the evening meal. Urias and Shelton had been out of the house all day. The children were busy playing. Katherine had spent four hours sewing, but making clothing for strangers gave her little joy.

All her life, her time had been owned by others. Her own goals and desires had diminished to the point where she felt like nothing more than cattle. *But at least I knew where I fit in.* Freedom without purpose left her feeling as if there were no solid ground under her feet.

Katherine strolled to the clearing in the woods, where she'd spent a lot of private time. The circular area contained two comfortable wooden benches. The large, flowering bushes that hedged the alcove gave a person some privacy in the spring and summer, though a person wouldn't remain hidden for long in the late fall. Grandma Mac had created the little sanctuary when she was a young bride living in this new territory. Grandma and Grandpa Mac moved to Jamestown five years before it was incorporated in 1827. At that time there were only a handful of neighbors. This small area had become a safe haven for all the women of the family. Katherine felt like family to the MacKenneths.

She sat on one of the benches and glanced at the sky. A pink dusting of clouds in the west made her realize she didn't have much time to be alone.

The crack of a falling tree in the distance made her jump. *Are the men still cutting down trees for winter?* She could have sworn Urias had said they'd cut all the cords of wood needed for their three households last week.

She listened carefully. No sound of chopping. Perhaps nature had taken its course on a lone tree in the woods. Katherine peeked her head out of the sanctuary and looked for any signs of the men. She saw no one.

Settling back on the bench, she prayed. It was in this garden she had rediscovered God and become acquainted with the concept of Jesus as her friend. A smile spread across her face as she remembered Grandma Mac telling her how foolish she'd been to blame God for her mother's actions or for the way she'd been treated by the men who had owned her. She'd never been able to tell Grandma Mac, or anyone else for that matter, the sordid details about her life as a bondservant. Grandma Mac was too godly of a woman to hear such things, she reasoned. Katherine wanted to shield all the family from such horrors.

Earlier that day, when memories of her horrible past had bubbled to the surface with intense urgency, she'd almost told Shelton the truth about her life. But she couldn't. No one should know. No one would respect her if they knew.

"Oh God, why?"

Another memory floated to the surface. Shelton holding her in his arms, his loving touch on her skin. The sweet caress of his finger on her face when he brushed the strands of her hair away from her eyes.

"How can this be, Lord? How can I desire a man when. . ." Tears spilled into her lap. "Forgive me, Lord. I am such a wretch."

"Child?" Grandma Mac's voice cracked.

Katherine looked up and saw the older woman shuffling toward her. She wiped the tears from her face. "I'm sorry. I'll let you have your prayer time." She stood.

Grandma Mac leaned on her cane, placing a hand on Katherine's shoulder. "I'll not hear a single word of you apologizing for praying here." She urged Katherine to sit back down, then joined her on the bench. "Now, tell me child, why all the tears?"

❧

Shelton led Kehoe to the trough. Sweating and snorting heavily from the fast run, the horse greedily lapped up the water.

"Fine horse, Greene." Mr. Crockett brought his horse to the water. "You sure I can't interest you in selling him?"

"Afraid not."

"I can see why you're holding on to him."

"He's sired some good stock. My mare should be foaling next month. Their mating should produce excellent offspring."

"Will that one be for sale?"

"More than likely, when the time is right. Interested?"

Mr. Crockett extended his hand. "Absolutely. Send word and I'll examine the foal."

Shelton shook the man's hand.

Crockett eyed Kehoe. "I've got a mare that might produce good stock with your stallion. Would you consider allowing me to hire him to stud?"

Shelton smiled. "I'm living with Urias O'Leary. When your mare is in season, send word to me through him, and Kehoe and I will come on over."

"Wonderful. Have you considered racing him professionally? Could earn you some additional income. And those events can be good exhibitions for getting the word out about the stud service."

"I'll keep that in mind." Shelton looked at the setting sun. "I'd best be getting home. Good night, Mr. Crockett."

"Good night, Mr. Greene." Mr. Crockett handed him his pay envelope.

Shelton stuffed it in his pocket. He had earned the man's respect, but only after he'd been fired. How could he send for his parents if he couldn't find gainful employment?

As he turned his horse toward home, his hands stung from the opened blisters. The idea of Katherine's gentle fingers on these fresh wounds sent a glimmer of emotion through him. But what emotion? The word *acceptance* came to mind. Was that what he was feeling? His father and mother had accepted his help with the family finances, but only after the bankers told Hiram there was no other alternative. Urias and Prudence showed genuine concern for him, but he didn't feel exactly at home in their house. The time had come for him to make his own mark in the world. But how?

Kehoe kept a gentle canter back to the farm. Shelton decided he needed to spend more time in prayer. Then he'd talk with Urias and see if he could come up with some ideas. With the pending stud fee and the sale of the foal, maybe he could convince the bank to give him a loan for his own farm. He had proof back in Hazel Greene of the profits he'd made from the breeding of his horses. Would that be enough for the bank to take a risk?

As he came up to the barn, he saw Urias loading his wagon with Katherine's belongings. A jolt of concern raced through his heart. "What's going on?"

seven

Katherine sat on her bed, perplexed at the events that had occurred over the past hour. When Grandma Mac found her in the garden sanctuary, she'd told the dear old woman how foolish she felt for wanting a little privacy, a place of her own. The next thing she knew, they were marching back to Urias's house and Grandma Mac was informing the family that Katherine was moving in with her. The family agreed it was a wonderful idea since Grandma Mac could use the company now that her husband had passed on.

"What can I carry out to the wagon?" Shelton appeared in her doorway, looking like an Irish warrior prepared to defend the honor of a maid.

"The quilt can go, but the rest of the bedding will stay here."

He held out his hands for the quilt. "Anything else?"

"Shelton," she cried out when she saw the wounds on his wonderful, sensitive hands. She ran to his side and examined the blisters more closely. "What happened?"

Shelton shuffled back and forth on his feet. "I've been working at Crockett's mill for a couple days. My hands aren't used to that kind of work."

"Let me cleanse them."

"They'll be fine." He tried to stuff them in his pockets, but quickly pulled them out again. "Why are you moving?"

"It was Grandma Mac's idea."

Prudence walked in. "And when Grandma Mac gets her mind bent on something. . ." She started folding up the quilt.

"Well, let's just say folks respect their elders here."

Katherine returned her attention to the wounds on Shelton's hands. "Did you wear gloves?" She took a cool compress and drizzled water over the wounds. Dirt and grit had worked their way into some of the open sores.

Urias appeared in the doorway. "He's a sensitive boy," he said with a smirk. Prudence giggled.

"I am not a boy," Shelton seethed. "And yes, I was wearing gloves."

"Just teasing. I know you've been working hard. Mr. Crockett makes a man do an hour and a half's work in an hour."

Shelton's shoulders relaxed. Katherine fought off the desire to rub the tension from his back. "He needs some udder salve. His hands are raw."

Urias stepped into the room and peered at Shelton's fingers. "You said you had blisters. You didn't tell me they looked like ground meat. Prudence, take care of Shelton. Katherine and I can finish packing. Grandma Mac will have my hide if I don't get Katherine's bed over there in the next fifteen minutes."

❧

By the time Katherine arrived at Grandma Mac's house, the rest of the MacKenneth family had set up one of the rooms for her. She couldn't imagine a more supportive family, or one that feared the matriarch so much.

Over the years Grandma Mac had spent a lot of time with Katherine, teaching her to read and schooling her in much of the education she'd missed growing up. Would rooming with her solve her desire to have her own place? She didn't think so. But a break from the late-night awakenings of baby Elizabeth would be a welcome relief.

After the rest of the family left for home, Katherine found

herself sitting on her bed in a strange room. She loved Grandma Mac and looked forward to helping her. It was becoming increasingly difficult for the dear woman to get around these days. Besides, for the first five years of Prudence and Urias's marriage, Katherine had been a part of their household. It would be nice for them to have time alone as a family. At least, that was what she kept telling herself.

A light tap on the door drew her out of her musings. "Yes?"

"May I come in, dear?"

"Of course."

Grandma Mac sat in the rocking chair beside the bed. "I suppose I acted a bit rash to have you move in with me this very evening. But there was a reason for my insistence."

Katherine clamped her mouth tight.

"The barn is not a fit place for Shelton to live. And adding a room on to Urias's house right now would not be wise because of the new baby. I proposed that you move in with me so Shelton can move into your old room."

"I see." She felt a bit embarrassed at not having thought of that herself. It made perfect sense.

"Also, Urias is quite concerned about your fear of Shelton. Although I haven't seen it myself for the past week or more."

"No, I'm not afraid of Shelton."

"Good. Because I'm hiring him to work for me while Mac takes his family fur trapping."

Katherine nodded. She wasn't frightened by Shelton any longer. At least not in the same way as before. Now she was just afraid of the emotions she felt toward him.

"Do you love him?"

Katherine's head shot up. "No."

"Hmm. That's an awfully quick reply for a woman who was crying out to God about her feelings for a man just a few hours ago."

"I can't love him." Katherine glided her hands over the quilt. "I'm not fit."

"Nonsense. You are a redeemed child of the King. You're as fit as any woman to marry a man."

"I can't. Besides, Shelton doesn't think of me in those terms. He knows who I am, who I was. After all, I was his servant."

"Tell me this, Katherine. Does Prudence treat you like a servant?"

She shook her head.

"Does Shelton?"

Did he really? "No, I suppose not."

Grandma Mac leaned back in the rocker and swung back and forth for a moment. "Then perhaps you should trust God and pray for His guidance. You've healed tremendously since you arrived five years ago. You no longer blame God. You've trusted Him with your soul. Why not trust Him regarding your future, too?"

How could she argue with that? "I will pray," she agreed.

"Good. Now, this old woman has stayed up way beyond her bedtime." Grandma Mac lifted herself from the chair and leaned on her cane as she shuffled out of the room. "Trust God, dear. And don't argue with Him."

Was she arguing with God? Did she truly trust Him? Trust was an issue she felt she'd never overcome.

Shelton's bloody palms came back to her mind. What about Shelton? Was he working in his own strength?

❧

After a couple of days, Shelton could work his hands with minimal pain. And a good thing, too. For today he would begin working for the senior Mrs. MacKenneth, feeding her livestock and doing some odds and ends around the place. Knowing his own limitations in farming, he'd insisted on a low wage, and thankfully, she agreed.

Planting and harvesting hay and other grains would be the hardest part. But if he were ever going to get his own place, he needed to learn how to maintain a farm. Maybe then he could get a banker to secure a loan with him to purchase his own farmstead.

The idea of working for Mrs. MacKenneth pleased him, but the thought of seeing Katherine every day increased his joy tenfold. *Father, help me win her heart.*

He rode Kehoe up to Grandma Mac's farm. He found Katherine in the yard, hanging linens on the line. A smile creased his lips. A desire to see her doing the same for him and their family one day gave him pause. He pictured her with two children hanging on to her skirts and a round belly full with another. Shelton shook off those thoughts. She wasn't ready. And although he was, he needed to keep focused on slowly building a relationship with her, one in which she didn't jump at his very presence.

"It's good to see you, Katherine."

A light blush rose on her cheeks. "How are your hands?"

"Much better, thank you. How's Mrs. MacKenneth?"

"Good, all things considered. I didn't realize she was having so much trouble getting around."

Shelton dismounted. "Did she fall?"

A gentle smile creased Katherine's face. "No. Just old bones, she says."

As much as he wanted to stay and talk with Katherine, that wasn't why he'd come. He couldn't afford to lose another job. "Excuse me, Katherine, but Mrs. MacKenneth is waiting on me."

He took the porch steps two at a time.

Half an hour later he was out in the barn with a list of chores. He couldn't imagine how Mac and Urias kept up their farms as well as Mrs. MacKenneth's. Perhaps this wasn't a token job offer after all. She really could use a part-time workman around the old house.

"Shelton," Katherine called from the barn door, "Grandma Mac says she expects you to join us for lunch."

"I take that to mean there isn't an option."

Katherine chuckled. "For an old woman she sure has some spit and fire."

"I believe you're right. Do you know where she keeps the whetstone?"

"No. I'm afraid I know little about the barn. I've only been in here a time or two. But I'll be glad to help you look."

"Thank you. I'm sure we can find it. If not, I can borrow Urias's."

She stepped inside and helped him search the barn. "Do you like farming?"

Shelton didn't quite know how to answer that question. "Truthfully, no. But there are a lot of things in this life that we have to do that aren't pleasant."

Katherine went rigid.

Shelton mentally kicked himself. He'd done it again, reminded her of the past. A past he prayed he was wrong about. He wanted to ask her straight out if she'd been abused but that would be rude. "I'm sorry. I didn't mean to speak insensitively. Forgive me."

She knitted her eyebrows and cocked her head. Her lips parted slightly, but she closed them again.

"Are you all right?"

She pressed her eyelids closed, then opened them slowly. For a moment he lost himself in those powerful green eyes that had captivated his dreams more nights than he could count.

"I'm fine. I apologize for responding so dramatically to a perfectly natural statement. What is it about farm life that you don't appreciate?"

He thought about her question for a moment. "To be honest, I guess I'm a bit spoiled. I was raised in a house where servants did my bidding. I'm not afraid of hard work, but my body hasn't done much of it. My hands protest every time I try to do something physical. I can't wait until the day when I can hire a man to do these tasks for me."

She peered at him, as if trying to determine what meaning lay behind his words.

"It's not that I find the work beneath me. I just don't like doing it. I will because I must, but it doesn't give me the same joy I find in training Kehoe and Kate."

Her eyes flew open. "You named your mare after me?"

Heat rose up his neck and covered his ears. "Yes," he confessed and went back to searching for the whetstone. He wanted to confess his love for her, but held back. Now was not the time.

"Shelton?" Her voice wavered.

He looked up at her. "Yes?"

"It's not possible." Katherine ran out of the barn.

A strong drive to run after her captured his heart. But his head kept his feet firmly planted. There would be opportunities in the future to speak with her, to convince her that they did in fact have a future. But he could not provide that future, not just yet.

❧

Katherine trembled as she yanked a large pot out of the kitchen cupboard. Why did every encounter with Shelton make her long to be in his arms? How could the simplest things he said make her want to confess her past to him? She wanted a future with him. But Hiram Greene had made it clear that she was not fit for his family. No, a relationship with Shelton was impossible.

"Nothing is impossible with God." The fragmented piece of

scripture rang in her head. "Lord, you don't understand." Katherine let out a mild cough. "That didn't come out right. But, Lord, You have no idea who Hiram Greene is." She cleared her throat again and set the pot on the stove with a clang. "Lord, I know You know all, but even You have to admit that man is. . ."

"Is what, dear?" Grandma Mac asked.

Katherine looked up and saw the older woman standing in the doorway.

"I didn't mean to interrupt your prayers, but if you keep banging those pans, there won't be one fit to fry in."

Katherine looked down. "I'm sorry."

Grandma Mac sat at the kitchen table. "Tell me, what's on your mind, child?"

Katherine took a tin measuring cup out of the drawer.

"Has Shelton Greene acted inappropriately toward you?"

"Shelton? He's the only man who's treated me like a woman."

"So you do love him."

"No," Katherine replied, a bit too quickly. "I respect him. Probably too much."

Grandma Mac narrowed her gaze. "Not all men behave badly, you know."

Katherine's hands shook. She put down the measuring cup and turned away from Grandma Mac's knowing gaze. The past blazed through her memory as quickly as a bolt of lightning in the sky.

Holding back tears, she faced Grandma Mac again. Her pale brown eyes spoke volumes.

Katherine sat beside the intuitive woman. "You know, don't you?" she whispered.

"I've suspected from the start. Whenever any man got within ten feet of you, your back stiffened. But you let your guard down around Shelton. At first I thought it was because he was family. Now I suspect you love him. But because of your past you don't feel you have the right to have a blessed union with a man. Am I right?"

Katherine nodded. "Yes. But there's more to it than that."

Grandma Mac lifted her chin. "You can tell me, dear."

"If I could ever truly love a man, it would be Shelton. But. . ."

"But what, honey?"

"When Shelton's father owned me, before I came to move here. . .just before Urias found me, five years ago. . .Mr. Greene made it very clear that he would never consent to a union between me and his son."

"I see. So because you were once their servant, you aren't allowed to love Shelton? Or do you think Shelton's father would disown him if he married you?"

"Family is very important to Shelton. I don't think I've had one conversation with him in which he didn't discuss his commitment to provide for and help his family. I could never stand in the way of that." Katherine stopped herself from saying more. Some things were best kept hidden.

"You are not Hiram Greene's servant, nor any other man's. You are God's child. And He loves you. He forgives you. His heart aches for the improprieties that have fallen upon you. But you are redeemed, Katherine. You're free to pursue a relationship with Shelton if that is what you wish. Is it?"

Katherine stared at the tabletop. "Honestly, I don't know. I do like Shelton, and I enjoy talking with him very much. But I don't know if I could ever trust a man enough to love him in. . .the way that God designed."

Grandma Mac patted her hand. "Unfortunately, other women have been in situations similar to yours. Some were able to move beyond the pain of the past and have good lives with loving husbands. Others have turned to wanton ways, believing they are worthless. Please don't think that about yourself. Walk in faith and trust God."

"I could never live a life of ill repute. But I don't see how it is possible for me to live with a man."

"By God's grace, dear." Grandma Mac rose from the chair and left Katherine alone with her thoughts.

Perhaps one day I could live with a man. But the likelihood of it being Shelton was slim. Hiram Greene stood like an ox in the barnyard—huge, strong, and stubborn to the point of being immovable.

eight

Shelton worked at Mrs. MacKenneth's farm every morning. During the afternoons he rode into Creelsboro to procure stud fees. He arranged for the setup to take place in the livery stable in Creelsboro. The client would bring in a mare, then Kehoe would come into the narrow corral and do his part, after which he returned to his own pen. Unfortunately, Kehoe had suffered once or twice. After the last service, Shelton had found him bleeding. The mare had bitten him hard on the neck.

After a couple of weeks, he had earned enough money to speak with a bank manager about securing a loan for purchasing his own property. He hoped there might be a foreclosure he could pick up for a reasonable rate.

Shelton left Kehoe in the public stable and headed for the bank. The streets were filled with travelers heading west. The excitement in the air promised hope and freedom. Shelton felt its powerful tug as an easy answer to his financial problems.

He stepped off the dusty street into the dark-paneled confines of the bank.

"Good afternoon." A bald, middle-aged man extended a hand to him. His pin-striped business suit draped over a stout figure.

"Afternoon," Shelton responded, accepting the handshake. "I was wondering if I could speak with the manager."

"That'd be me, sir. Reynolds is the name. What can I do for you?"

"I'd like to talk about getting a loan to purchase some property in the area."

The man lit up like a full moon. "Why don't we step into my office."

Two hours later Shelton came out with a smile on his face and a lightness in his heart. Mr. Reynolds had said that once he verified Shelton's past financial dealings with the banks back in Hazel Greene, he didn't see a problem giving him a loan. He even recommended a two-hundred-acre farm where the owner had passed away and the widow hoped to return to family in New York.

Two hundred acres seemed like more than Shelton required. Then again, the horses needed grazing fields and long, open runs for strength and development. He had a lot to think about and a lot to pray about.

He sent a letter to his parents to let them know of the recent turn of events. Soon he'd be able to write and tell them where their new home would be. A desire to share his news with Katherine spurred him on. He urged Kehoe to move a bit faster. He looked at the wound on the horse's neck. It had begun to bleed again. Shelton pulled back on the reins and let the stallion trot at a nice even pace.

As he neared the outskirts of the MacKenneths' farm, the sun was beginning to set. Katherine would have to wait until tomorrow to hear his good news. He enjoyed seeing her every day at the elder MacKenneth's farm, but he missed spending time with her and the family at Urias's. The way her face lit up when she played with her nephews made his heart soar. *I think we should have a large family.*

"Whoa," he said out loud, quickly reining in his thoughts.

Kehoe pulled to an abrupt stop. Shelton clicked his tongue to encourage the animal to continue. "Sorry, boy. I wasn't talking to you."

He chided himself for allowing his imagination to stray into foolish territory. He couldn't convince her to open up to him, let alone kiss him, and here he was picturing having children with her.

When he arrived at Urias's barn, he removed Kehoe's saddle, brushed him down, and carefully washed the wound on the horse's neck. Then he checked on Kate. He gave the mare a good brushing.

"Do you always spend this much time with them?" Katherine asked.

Startled, he raised his head suddenly and nearly crowned it on the side of the pen. "What are you doing here?"

"I was invited to dinner, and Urias sent me out to fetch you to join us. The children have all eaten, but Urias is getting hungry and cranky."

Shelton chuckled. "I'm sorry. I didn't know they were holding dinner on me. I had to tend to Kehoe's injury."

Katherine came up to the stallion. "What happened?"

"A frisky mare bit him."

"Oh." A gentle blush covered Katherine's cheeks. "Is Kate almost ready to foal?"

"Any time now." Shelton put down the brush and washed his hands at the pump. "I have some good news."

Katherine smiled. The glow of her green eyes and the gentle rose pink of her lips warmed Shelton deep within.

He switched his focus back to the ice-cold water from the pump. "Mr. Reynolds at the bank said that if my references and facts concerning my bank records in Hazel Greene check out, I'll be approved for a loan to purchase a farm in the area."

"Oh Shelton, that's wonderful news." Katherine wrapped her arms around him, then immediately pulled away.

He knew he couldn't pressure her to show affection, but inwardly he rejoiced that she had reached out to him. "I sent a letter to my parents and let them know it won't be much longer before they can plan on moving here."

All the energy in Katherine's face disappeared. "I'm happy for you."

If that was happy, what would describe her earlier reaction? "Katherine, Father's changed. He's a humbled man."

She gave a weak smile and a nod. "Dinner is ready whenever you are."

Shelton watched her walk off toward the house. He kicked the pump with his foot. His toe throbbed. That would teach him to take out his anger on an immoveable object.

"Father God," he prayed, "am I so blinded by love for Katherine that I'm ignoring the problems our union would create for my parents? And for her?" Shelton sighed. "Your will, Father, not mine." He hoped he meant his prayer, because he knew his heart would be destroyed if he and Katherine would never be together.

❧

Katherine sat numbly through dinner. Shelton's news flooded the conversation. Urias spoke of some farms in the area that might be available for a good price. Shelton mentioned one where a woman was recently widowed. Having lived with Grandma Mac for a short time, Katherine realized how hard it would be for an elderly woman to live alone and maintain a farm, even a small one such as Grandma Mac now owned. Rather than a farm, Shelton wanted a ranch, where he could breed horses.

The conversation moved on to other news from the area, but the lively chatter didn't engage her. She wondered how big a ranch he would have. And whether he would feel so compelled to provide for his parents that they would live on the property with him.

Urias's voice broke through her jumbled thoughts. "I read somewhere they moved Daniel Boone and his wife's bones to

Frankfort on September thirteenth. The town had a parade and everything."

"Seems odd to move a man's bones after he's been laid to rest," Prudence said. "But I imagine the state is happy to have the man who blazed the trail to Kentucky back home."

Prudence peered at Katherine. "You're awfully quiet tonight."

"I suppose I don't have much to offer in a discussion about local affairs."

"I'd be interested in anything you had to say." Shelton set his fork on the table. "What were you thinking about while we were discussing Daniel Boone?"

She'd done it this time. She should have known Shelton would be able to tell she was distracted by her own thoughts.

Everyone at the table stared at her, waiting for her response. *All right,* she thought. *If he really wants to know. . .*

"I just find it hard to understand why you feel the need to provide for your parents. I suppose not having my own parents any longer, I don't understand your loyalty to them."

Shelton wiped his lips with his napkin. "It's a question of honor. I don't approve of my father's actions, but I am duty bound by God's Word and my conscience to honor my parents."

Urias reached for his glass of water. "I have to agree. Hiram Greene isn't one of my favorite people in the world, but he is Prudence's father, and I choose to respect him because he raised my beautiful wife." He looked at Prudence, who smiled lovingly at him. Then he returned his attention to Katherine. "What would you do if our mother showed up one day? Would you curse her and throw her out, or would you forgive her and provide her with a place to stay?"

"Seeing as how I don't own my own home, I couldn't make such an offer." *And I probably never will be able to anyway.* "I honestly don't know what I'd do if Mother were to show up."

"I'd have a problem with that as well," Shelton acknowledged.

"I think we all would," Prudence offered. "While my parents had their problems, they did love us and raise us well."

Katherine sat back in her chair and thought on that for a moment. The Greens did love their children. And that was more than she could say about her mother.

Prudence reached for Urias's hand. He wrapped his fingers around hers. "Father knows he tricked us and used us. I don't think he will ever ask for forgiveness, even though we gave it to him long ago."

Katherine forked a piece of meat but couldn't raise it to her mouth. "Forgiveness is one thing. But taking care of them? Hiram Greene is not so old that he can't take care of himself."

"Father's gambling is like a sickness. He can't seem to stop. And Mother shouldn't suffer for his transgressions. So I will provide for them. In my mind it isn't an option; it is an obligation I must fulfill to be an honorable man to God."

Katherine nibbled her lower lip. "I guess it's my own bitterness that can't allow me to see why you feel so strongly about this. I don't know if I'll ever get over being owned by others."

"If Hiram Greene hadn't acquired your bond," Urias interjected, "I wouldn't have found you. I wouldn't have found my beautiful wife either. And I wouldn't have three of the most adorable children on the face of the earth. I wish things had been different for you, Katherine, but they weren't. Even though you lived through harsh times, you need to accept the facts and move on with the blessings God has given you."

"I guess," she added with a sigh, "if it wasn't for Hiram Greene, I wouldn't have my freedom and a cherished family."

Shelton smiled.

And I wouldn't have Shelton in my life, she added silently. Was Grandma Mac right? Could she have a future with him? Katherine picked up her fork and ate the now-cold chunk of meat. "Forgive me for being so rude, Shelton."

"You're always free to speak your mind around me."

She appreciated the freedom he gave her. But to live under the same roof as Hiram Greene again? That would take a double portion of God's grace.

The conversation shifted to Grandma Mac. Prudence served a delicious apple pie for dessert.

Stuffed, Katherine pushed back from the table. "I'd better help you with these dishes and get on my way or Grandma Mac might wonder why I was gone so long."

"Nonsense. Urias promised to help me in the kitchen."

Urias's eyebrows shot up. "Shelton, would you be so kind as to escort Katherine back to Grandma Mac's?"

"Be my pleasure." Shelton wiped his mouth with the cloth napkin and placed it neatly next to his dish.

He is such a gentleman, Katherine thought wistfully. "I can go by myself."

"Indulge me," Urias said. "I saw some bear tracks earlier this morning."

"All right." Katherine knew about Urias's encounters with bears. His first had occurred when he was thirteen. A smile edged her lips as she remembered the tale of her frightened brother sitting backward on the horse while the bear made itself at home in Mac and Pamela's wagon. Her smile disappeared when she remembered another occasion. Mac had barely survived the attack from the bear that killed his first wife.

"Should we secure the livestock?" Shelton asked.

"You might want to close up the hen house and bring Grandma Mac's pig into the barn for the night," Urias suggested.

"Absolutely. What about Mac and Pam's place?"

"I secured it before dinner." Urias got up and carried some dinnerware to the kitchen. "Good night, Katherine. It was nice having you at our table again."

Katherine smiled. "It was good to be here."

They said their good-byes and Shelton escorted Katherine out the front door.

❧

Shelton placed his hand in the small of Katherine's back as they walked down the porch stairs together. He felt a slight flinch from her, but she relaxed a moment later. It had been a forward move, but it felt right.

"Look at all those stars," she declared with awc and wonder, gazing at the sky.

"God sure knows how to paint a pretty canvas, doesn't He?"

"It's magnificent." Katherine tightened her coat a notch. "I'm sorry if I offended you tonight."

"I love your straightforward honesty."

They continued to walk in the direction of Grandma Mac's house. "Shelton, there are things you don't know about me."

He weighed whether or not to ask, but decided to wait on her. "There are things you don't know about me, too, Katherine." *Like how much I love you. How much I want to wrap you in my arms and protect you. And what happened when I was sent away from you.*

"Name one thing," she challenged.

He decided to change the mood. "When I was seven, I ran away from home."

"How far did you get?"

"The neighbors' house. I didn't know how to get anywhere else."

Katherine laughed. "What did your parents do?"

"My father tanned my hide. My mother hugged me until I thought I'd break in two. Personally, I preferred my father's response. It was quick, and over in a minute. My mother kept hugging me for the next three days. At seven a boy doesn't want to be hugged a lot." *Unlike the man now standing beside you.*

"I have seen that same reaction in Mac and Pamela's boys. Didn't you appreciate the affection?"

"Of course. But I couldn't let Mother see that."

"Did you ever consider running away from home again?"

"No, not really." He slowed the pace. "Remember when I was sent away, right before Urias found you?"

"Yes." She stiffened. He kept his hand in the small of her back.

"If Father hadn't sent me away, I might have run off then. I was so angry with him. He was being totally unreasonable. But looking back, I think I was being unreasonable as well. I was only sixteen at the time. That was pretty young to. . ."

"To what?"

"I told him I loved you and that I would marry you the next time the parson came around."

Katherine stopped in her tracks. "You did what?"

He gazed at her face, bathed in the moonlight. The sight made his heart pound and his palms sweat. "You're even more beautiful now than when you were seventeen."

"Shelton, please don't."

"Don't what? Tell you that I love you? That I've always loved you, from the first moment you came to my home?"

Tears ran down her cheeks. She trembled.

He stepped toward her, opening his arms, willing her to come to him. Katherine eased forward and leaned into his chest.

"My dear, sweet Katherine." He held her gently in his arms. He inhaled the wonderful scent that was hers alone. *Lord, give me strength.*

"I'm damaged," she sobbed.

He held her tighter. *Lord, I wish I could take away her pain.* "Do you want to tell me about it?"

She shook her head.

"That's all right, sweetheart. Whenever you're ready." Shelton closed his eyes and held the woman he loved. For the first time, she'd come to him, willingly, openly. He would cherish this moment for as long as he lived. He kissed her gently on top of her red curls.

"I thought I was nearly free from the past," she choked out. "But since you came back I've been having nightmares. I never completely stopped having them, but they've been more frequent since you arrived."

"I'm so sorry. I never meant to hurt you."

"I feel dirty for liking you," she confessed.

He cradled her head in his hands and encouraged her to look at him. "My dear, sweet Katherine, I love you. What happened in the past couldn't be your fault."

Katherine pulled away. "You don't understand."

"Tell me so I will," he pleaded.

"I can't," she cried, and bolted toward Grandma Mac's farmhouse.

He ran after her. *I pushed too hard.* "Katherine, stop. Please!"

She stumbled. He caught her. He held her gently, fighting the desire to kiss her and hold on to her until she saw and felt how much he loved her. "Whenever you're ready, you can come to me. I will not force you. I respect you too much to make you do something you don't want to do."

"You have no idea," she mumbled.

nine

Katherine kept to herself for the next three days. Spending time with Shelton was dangerous to her soul. She desired to be in his arms. She ached to kiss him. But she couldn't give in to such temptations, even if Grandma Mac did say God gave those desires for the holy purposes of marriage. She knew in her mind that was the truth. But she had no way to know whether she would respond positively to his kiss or if the ugly past would come back and taint the love she felt for Shelton. She didn't want to soil something as precious as his love for her and hers for him.

Not that she'd confessed her feelings for him yet.

She sat in her bedroom, working on her sewing. She'd sold several shirts to the mercantile and had an order for a dozen more.

"Katherine," Shelton's voice called out from behind the door. "May I come in?"

She set aside her sewing and opened the door. "What can I do for you?"

"I could use a favor, if you don't mind."

"What is it?"

"I'm wondering if you can take care of Mrs. MacKenneth's livestock for the next two days."

"I could try." She wanted to ask why he couldn't do it, but didn't feel she had the right to.

"Thank you. Can I show you where I keep everything?"

"Please." She followed him out of the house.

In the barn, Shelton showed her the sacks of grain and

instructed her in how Grandma Mac liked to mix her pig slop. "Any questions?" he asked.

"Nope. Looks pretty straightforward."

"I appreciate this. I'll be happy to pay you for your time."

Katherine placed her hands on her hips.

Shelton laughed. "I didn't think so, but I was duty bound to offer."

"You have a strong sense of duty and honor, don't you?"

"I get that from my father. I know it doesn't make sense, with his gambling and all, but he wasn't always irresponsible. He taught us that a man's word isn't worth anything if he doesn't back it up with his actions. I know you've only known my father when he was gambling, but there is another side to him."

"Urias made sense the other night when he said you and Prudence wouldn't be the people you are today if not for how your parents raised you."

Shelton opened his arms but she didn't step into his embrace. "Katherine, I've missed you."

She looked at the hay on the floorboards and brushed it aside with her foot. "I've missed you, too."

"I apologize if confessing my love for you made you uncomfortable."

"There's precious little you can do that won't make me uncomfortable. But it's not you; it's me. Eventually, I will not be as uneasy around you."

Shelton's smile sent her heart beating faster.

"So, where are you going that you need someone to help with the livestock?" she asked, eager to change the subject.

"Urias is taking me fur trapping. He's going to show me how to set traps, how to maintain them, and how to skin and prepare the hides. He and Mac bring in a little extra income that way. Once I purchase my own land, I'll need to know what I can hunt and what is marketable."

"Any more signs of the bear?"

"Not that we've seen or heard about. Hopefully it went back to the woods." Shelton leaned against a post supporting the upper loft and chewed on a piece of hay.

"You're looking pretty relaxed today," she observed.

"I am. I feel like my prayers are finally being answered. I should hear from the bank soon. I've been looking at some properties, but so far I haven't found one I'm excited about."

"What are you looking for?"

"Enough land for the horses to run and graze. Also enough to grow the grain for their feed. Hopefully a property with a house already built on it. Otherwise, my parents won't be able to move out here until next spring. I'm not sure they'll make it through the winter in Hazel Greene."

Katherine stiffened. A knot the size of a feed bucket tightened in her stomach. "I still find it hard to believe that your father squandered away all his money."

"You're not the only one. It's so out of character that he'd get caught up in gambling. He taught Prudence and me to be wise with our money. I guess sin is an all-consuming thing."

"How does one know the difference between sin and love?" Katherine covered her mouth with her hands. She hadn't meant to say that.

"Are you ready to talk about the past?"

She shook her head.

"Then let's not attempt to answer that question now. Later will be soon enough."

"Shelton, its not you."

"It's not you either, Katherine. It's sin that's been done to you."

Katherine balled her hands into fists. "Do you know?"

"I suspect—because of how afraid you are of men—that

one or more. . .took liberties with you."

Katherine nodded and choked back tears.

"When you're ready to tell me about it, I'll be here. In the meantime, know that I'm praying for you, that I love you, and that nothing that happened to you will change my love for you."

"I don't deserve you." She sniffed.

Shelton opened his arms. She snuggled into his embrace. "You deserve better than me, Katherine. You're sweet and precious and I love you."

"I love you, too," she whispered into his chest.

❧

Shelton didn't want to let her go. However, Urias was waiting on him. He hated the thought of leaving, especially now that Katherine was opening up her heart to him. But he had no choice.

He pulled slightly away from her. "So, have you ever helped a horse deliver a foal?"

"No." Her gentle curls brushed under his chin. She stepped out of his embrace. "Are you concerned about Kate?"

"She's showing signs that she's about to deliver. She's done it before, so there shouldn't be any problems. But if it happens while I'm off fur trapping. . ."

"Perhaps you should tell Urias you'd prefer to go another time. He'll understand."

"I'm certain he will. But I want to have enough money—"

Katherine finished his sentence. "—to purchase your land."

He shrugged.

"What's of more value to you, the foal or a few furs?"

"If you put it that way, the foal." He looked out past the open doors of the barn.

"You need to be near Kate, just in case."

He looked back at her. "You're right."

"Remain focused on the overall plan."

Shelton smiled. "Besides being beautiful, you're a smart woman. I like that."

Katherine wagged her head back and forth. "You're impossible."

"Me?"

"And a real charmer. I bet all the ladies back in Hazel Greene found you quite appealing."

His own past flashed before his eyes. As much as he wanted to tell Katherine about it, the time wasn't right. He decided to keep the moment light. "I can turn on the charm when I want to. But those women all bored me." He winked. "I've been stuck on an Irish lass from my youth."

Katherine blushed. "How can you be so certain about. . ." she whispered.

"Us?"

She acknowledged with a nod.

"I wasn't, until I saw you again. I've been praying for five years, Katherine. I didn't know if my love was simply a child's fantasy or a real connection. Now that I've come to know you, I'm convinced this is real. However, I don't believe we can rush into a courtship. As much as I'd love to take you in my arms and rush off to the parson, there is a time and place for us. I'm willing to wait. Are you?"

Katherine took in a deep breath and let it out slowly. "I don't know how to answer that. Until last week I honestly didn't believe I was fit for marriage. Grandma Mac is challenging me to remember God's redemption and His forgiveness. I'm trying to hold on to that. I've lived a long time thinking I was worthless."

"My sweet Katherine, you are worth more than rubies or finely spun gold. You are precious in God's eyes and in mine, and I cherish your wisdom. I like discussing my plans with you. No one has ever listened to me and my ideas the way you do."

"I find your plans fascinating."

"You're the first person I wanted to tell about the bank coming through on the loan. Not my parents, not Urias and Prudence, but you. I want you to be a part of my future. Would you do me the honor of looking over the land and properties I'm most interested in? I'd very much like your opinion."

"You want me to help you decide on your property?"

"I'm hoping eventually it will be our property. I'm not looking for a commitment right now. I am planning for you to be my wife one day. But I believe we have a lot of work ahead of us before that can happen."

"What kind of work?"

"Things like my being able to take your hand without you pulling away from me. Time is the best healer, and you have to learn to trust me, slowly and surely." *In much the same way that I tame an unbroken horse.* "I'm willing to wait. We have time. Just be honest with me, and share your heart when you're ready to."

"I've never met a man so honest about his feelings."

"I've never been this honest before. You bring it out in me, Katherine. You're good for me in so many ways. I just pray I'm helpful to you as well."

A single tear fell from her eye. "You are."

He opened his arms and waited for her to walk into his embrace. Slowly she leaned into him and he cradled her in his arms. He inhaled that fresh scent that was uniquely hers. One day he'd be able to reach out and capture her in his arms. But it would take time to earn Katherine's trust. And with God's grace, he could wait.

❧

Katherine wiped the tears from her eyes as she rose from her knees after spending time with God, talking to Him about all that had happened that day. Shelton wanted to marry her. She'd known it before. In fact, she wanted it herself. But some part of her didn't. *How long before I can trust Shelton, Lord?*

Katherine dressed and went down to the kitchen. Preparing breakfast for herself and Grandma Mac didn't take half the time it took to prepare for Urias's family.

"Good morning, dear. Did you sleep well?"

"Yes, thank you. How are you today?" Katherine placed the eggs in boiling water to poach them.

"As fit as a woman can be when her bones ache just walking. Feels like a storm's brewing. An early winter storm, if my joints are correct."

"Anything I can do to help prepare?"

"I don't think so. We've been keeping the chickens in the coop at night since Urias spotted those bear tracks. Mac'll take care of things. Now, tell me how your conversation with Shelton went yesterday when you two were in the barn together."

Katherine chuckled. "You don't miss much, do you?"

"Not much. You looked happy, but as if the world was resting on your shoulders."

"He wants to marry me."

Grandma Mac's eyes twinkled. "Well, praise the Lord! Did you say yes?"

"He didn't ask me." Katherine pulled the toast off the grill and strained the poached eggs, placing one on each slice of bread. The smell of the wheat toast stirred up her hunger. Grandma Mac's favorite morning breakfast had become Katherine's as well.

"I'm confused."

"You're not the only one." Katherine explained how Shelton hoped they would marry one day, but he expected it to take some time before she was ready.

"Does he know about your past?"

"I haven't told him any details, but he figured it out, just like you did. I must be wearing a sign around my neck that says DAMAGED."

"Hardly." Grandma Mac shook some salt and pepper over her egg. "It's clear to those who love and care about you."

She knew she would one day have to tell Shelton the horrid details of the past if they were going to have a future together. She'd deal with that later, and with God's grace she would somehow manage to tell him.

"Tell me, have you and Shelton kissed?"

Katherine sat back. Heat spread across her cheeks. "No. I can't even hold the man's hand yet."

"I see."

Did she? Katherine certainly didn't understand her own fear. "I've sought comfort in his arms, though," she confessed.

Grandma Mac beamed. "And it was comforting?"

"Like nothing else I've experienced before."

"Ah, child. I do believe Shelton is right; you will be married one day. Now, eat up. You've got to deliver those shirts to Creelsboro today. I asked Mac to send Shelton over to escort you."

"You are a matchmaker."

"No, dear. God is the matchmaker. I'm simply providing moments when the two of you can talk and get to know each other." She gave the table two light taps.

As Katherine ate her eggs, peace covered her like a blanket. God's peace. Forgiving peace. Contented peace, like she'd always hoped to feel one day.

"You know, holding a man's hand is mighty satisfying if it's the right man." Grandma Mac grinned. "I loved my husband with a passion that grew as we aged."

Katherine blushed. "How can you talk about such things so freely?"

"God spoke about married love in the Bible. I figure if the good Lord saw fit to write about it, I might as well be willing to speak about it when the occasion arises." She sighed. "After Nash—Mac, as you know him—had his first marriage fail, my husband and I decided we should be honest and open with our children about love and relationships. Nash's first wife married him for his money, or the money she thought he had. They never got along. Over the years, she became a different person. Oh, I'm sure Nash did some things to provoke her. I'm not saying my son was totally innocent. But that woman, God rest her soul, could never be happy."

"Thank you, Grandma Mac. You're helping me a lot."

"You're welcome, dear. Now, finish your eggs. Shelton will be here shortly."

ten

Shelton stretched. He'd been up all night with Kate. If the foal didn't crown soon, he'd have to reach in and take it out.

"Shelton," Katherine called from just inside the barn door.

"I'm in Kate's stable." In a flash, he recalled promising Grandma Mac he'd pick Katherine up and take her into town that morning. "Oh no. I forgot about our trip today. I'm sorry."

"Don't worry about it." Katherine leaned over the rail of Kate's stable. "How's she doing?"

"She's been in labor all night."

"How can I help?"

Shelton glanced at her vivid green Sunday morning church dress. "Not in those clothes."

"I'll go back into the house and change. Anything else you need while I'm there?"

"Hot water for me to wash with."

A sudden deluge poured out of Kate. The mare stomped her hoof and her eyes grew wide. "It's all right, girl." Shelton patted the horse's flank.

"I'll be right back with that water."

As Katherine fled for the barn door, the foal's nose emerged. "You're doing fine, Kate." The front legs emerged. Shelton gently pulled the foal out.

"It's a boy!" The colt had Kehoe's black coat and Kate's markings. He was a good blend of the two horses.

The mare shifted on wobbly legs. She stared at the foal for a moment, then continued to pace in the stall. "What's the matter, girl?"

Her belly seemed too extended for having just given birth. Was there a problem with the placenta? Just then another nose crowned. "Twins!" Shelton smiled, then moved the newborn out of the way of Kate's determined pacing.

By the time Katherine returned with the bucket of water, Shelton was rubbing Kate down with some clean rags.

"Twins," she squealed. "Oh, Shelton, they're beautiful."

"They sure are. And Kate is a wonderful mother."

Kate cleaned up the foals and nudged them to their feet. Shelton finished washing down the new mother and then sponged himself down.

Katherine watched in awe. "I can't believe they both came out of her. It doesn't seem possible."

"It's amazing, isn't it? The miracle of birth fascinates me every time I witness it. God certainly chose an interesting way to bring new life into the world."

"Are they boys or girls?"

"One of each. A colt and a filly."

Shelton watched Katherine stare at the twin foals. He wondered if she were thinking about their children one day. *Don't push it,* he reminded himself. As easy as it was to tell Katherine he could be a patient man, he knew he'd have to fight impulse after impulse. Like right now. He wanted to come up beside her and wrap his arm around her. But he had to wait on Katherine. He would not spook her, no matter how much he wanted them to share every precious moment of life together.

He groaned inwardly. He was beginning to sound like a philosopher or poet. His father would have a few words about that, no doubt. No matter what he told himself or Katherine, he had to face the reality that their union would bring a harsh response from Hiram Greene. *Lord, please continue to change him, to soften him.*

"What's happening?" Urias asked from the doorway of the barn.

"Twins." Katherine beamed.

Urias ran to Kate's pen. "God's blessing you, Shelton. You've just doubled your income."

Shelton grinned. "I'm thinking of keeping the filly and selling the colt. On the other hand, the sale of both might be beneficial. I should pray on the matter."

"Ah yes. The quick dollar or the long, slow profit. Hard choices. How's Kehoe doing?" Urias glanced at the stallion's pen.

"His neck is healing well."

"Excellent." Urias leaned against the barn wall. "Mac says that bear was back on the property last night. Got one of the sheep my nephew was raising. Unless Mac and I can find him today, we need you to stay close and protect the women and children tonight."

"Be happy to."

Urias slapped him on the back. "Keep up the good work." He nodded at the newborns, then sauntered out of the barn.

Shelton yawned and stretched his weary muscles.

"If you're going to be up guarding the houses tonight," Katherine said, "you'd better get some rest."

"I'd like to, but I have chores to do."

"I'll take care of them for you. What do you need done?"

He started to protest. But she wouldn't hear of it. He succumbed to her willingness to help him and went to bed. The last thought in his mind was how Katherine's face had glowed while witnessing the new life of the foals.

❧

Katherine rushed around the barn, taking care of Shelton's chores. She enjoyed watching the new mother with her young. She still couldn't get over twins. She fought the desire to wake up Shelton to talk with him, but he needed his rest.

As she worked she prayed that Urias and Mac would find the bear today. This time of year bears ate anything they could get their paws on to build up for their hibernation period. The children would have to stay close to the house, and the twin foals would be a huge temptation. She was glad Shelton now had her old room in the house.

A renewed desire to be a mother one day surfaced with such intensity that she could no longer remain in the barn. She worked her way back toward Grandma Mac's house as soon as she finished Shelton's chores.

She didn't really want to face Grandma Mac and her perceptive ways. Things Katherine had kept hidden for years came out in the presence of that woman, though Katherine wasn't sure why. She considered going to the garden sanctuary, but fear of the bear kept her away.

Katherine stopped mid-stride. *Where can I go?* Again, an overwhelming desire for her own place took root.

Then she recalled Shelton's comment about his hope that his property would be hers one day. *Is that really possible?* There was no denying the sense of security she felt in his arms—a calmness she'd never known. There was something about laying her head on his chest that was so. . .relaxing.

"Lord, give me strength to overcome the evils that have befallen me. You know my pain and my shame. Please help me love Shelton the way You designed a man and woman to love each other."

She took one uncertain step forward. Fear over the desire she had just confessed circled around like a vulture waiting for the kill. Katherine collapsed onto her knees and wept. Bondage still held her. "Father God, please," she cried, "remove this fear."

She cupped her hands to her face and repeated the prayer over and over. Exhausted, she waited in the stillness that surrounded her. A gentle peace slowly began to fill her. Katherine wiped her eyes and stood. The fresh earthen scent of rich soil and pine needles invigorated her. The world around her seemed suddenly bright. Was she finally free? She took a tentative step forward, then another. Her back straightened with a surge of confidence. Her strides sure, she marched up to Grandma Mac's house.

She told the old woman the news of the twin foals and let her know that she would be going to Creelsboro that day. Grandma Mac questioned her, but Katherine found the inner strength to firmly yet politely tell her that she simply had business in town. An hour later she was on the road with the newest order for the mercantile.

"Good afternoon, Mr. Hastings," Katherine greeted the shopkeeper as she entered the store. The wooden shelves and bins were full. Various tools hung on the right wall. Perishable items were close to the counter in the back part of the store. A basket of fresh eggs sat near the register with rows of glass jars filled with brightly colored candy sticks. "I've completed the next order."

"Wonderful. I'm down to the last shirt. I'll need a dozen more as soon as possible. And could I get a few blouses for the ladies?"

"Do you have the material?" Katherine no longer paid for the fabric. She and Mr. Hastings had bartered. In exchange for free fabric Mr. Hastings paid a reduced price for the finished products.

"There are some light yellow, pink, and white cotton bolts over there. Take whatever you need."

"Thank you." Katherine walked to the fabric area. A bolt of beautiful ivory satin stood against the wall.

Mr. Hastings came over with his sheers. "Do you believe they sent that? I can't see me selling more than a yard or two for christening outfits. Brides don't marry in fancy getups here like they do back East. My supplier didn't even charge me for it. Would you like some?"

Katherine's eyes sparkled. "You wouldn't mind?"

"Not at all. In fact, why don't I keep four yards and give you the rest? I honestly don't think I'll be able to sell even the four yards."

"Thank you." Katherine thought of all the things she could do with that fabric. She could use some to make beautiful pillows for Christmas gifts, adding a special touch with some embroidery.

Then an image floated into her mind. Herself in a wedding gown made of this very material. Katherine's foot faltered.

Mr. Hastings reached out and caught her. "Are you all right?"

"I'm fine. My heel must have caught on the floorboard."

He released her.

"I'd like three yards each of the white, pink, and yellow cotton for the women's blouses you spoke of. Also, twenty yards of red flannel for the men's shirts. And as much of the ivory silk as you'd like to give me."

"Very good. Take your time and browse through the store. I just received some new shipments. Took in some wares from the folks heading west, too. Most of those items won't sell, but I feel sorry for those women who packed all their precious china, only to discover how impractical it is for the trip."

Katherine glanced over the myriad assorted wares. The mercantile carried a wide variety of things, from heavy tools to dainty teacups.

"How about some spools of thread?"

"Yes, please." Katherine eyed a set of china dishes with a pattern of a horse and a lady. She thought of Shelton. "How much for this set?"

"Fifteen dollars. But for you, I'll call it even with the shirts you brought in today."

"Are you certain?"

"Absolutely." He raised his right eyebrow. "For your dowry, perhaps?"

Katherine blushed.

❧

Shelton woke up just in time for dinner. He couldn't believe he'd slept the day away. He checked on Kate and the foals, ate dinner with the women and children, then prepared his rifle for his evening watch of the property. Once the family was secure for the night, he began his rounds, keeping watch over the pens close to the houses.

Katherine had seemed preoccupied at dinner. Apparently the shirts she'd been making had been selling so well that Mr. Hastings increased his order to include women's blouses. The ladies went on and on about them all night. As far as he was concerned, one blouse was as good as another. He'd seen plenty of finery in Hazel Greene; it didn't impress him much. He had never really fit in with "high society," as his father liked to call it. There was something refreshingly honest about people who worked off the land. Clothing was functional. Back home, women had closets larger than some of the bedrooms here. He definitely liked this simpler life.

Shelton guffawed out loud at the irony. *Life is not simpler out here. Whoever coined that phrase should have his head examined.*

There was one thing about life in Hazel Greene that he did prefer, however, and that was the use of coal for cooking and heating. It lasted longer than wood and didn't require all that chopping.

He decided to sit in a central location between the three houses to listen for any trouble. He leaned against a large boulder that marked the borders of the three properties and waited.

The sky darkened quickly after the sun went down. A chilly wind licked the back of his neck. Shelton pulled up the lapels on his woolen coat.

Crack. A twig snapped behind him. He reached for his rifle and turned.

"Shelton, where are you?" Katherine called softly.

Shelton lowered the rifle. "Over here."

She slowly emerged from the darkness.

"What are you doing out here?"

"I wanted to talk with you."

Shelton wagged his head. "Sometimes you do very foolish things." He pointed to his rifle. "Don't you realize how dangerous this is?"

Her eyes widened. "I'm sorry. I couldn't wait until morning."

"You're here now. What did you want to talk about?"

"Nothing specific, really. We just haven't had any time since this morning and. . ." Her words trailed off.

"I missed you, too." He opened his arms. "Come here."

She stepped into his embrace. He inhaled deeply. *Lord, I love this woman.*

She pulled back slightly and looked up at him. "I had a revelation. Well, I think it was a revelation. I was crying out to God today about my fear of love, and I decided to walk in faith. Then, as I stepped forward, I felt incredible crushing fear, like I have in the past. I prayed for God to remove it, and after a few moments, a gentle peace washed over me."

"Praise the Lord! That's wonderful."

"I've done that before, but this time God's peace felt a lot stronger. Or maybe I'm more confident in trusting it. I don't know. But the oddest thing happened at the mercantile this afternoon. While I was there, my footing slipped and Mr. Hastings reached out and caught me from falling. In the past, I would have jumped out of my skin. This time I didn't react at all. It seemed perfectly natural. I knew he wasn't trying to take advantage of me, but simply offering a helping hand."

"Oh, Katherine, I'm so happy for you. God is healing you."

"Yes. And for the first time, I feel worthy of it. Thanks to you."

"I'm glad. Now, tell me about the twins. I missed their first hours. How did they respond to their mother?"

Katherine leaned beside him against the rock and told him about the first hours of life for the new foals. Kate was a good mother; she'd raised a foal before. Shelton knew she'd do well with the twins.

He wanted to ask Katherine how many children she would like to have one day, but reminded himself that he had promised to take their relationship slowly.

"Katherine, would you be willing to look over a piece of property with me tomorrow?"

"I have a lot of sewing to do."

He felt her wall of resistance spring up again. "That's fine. I just thought I'd ask."

They sat together for a while in silence. "Shelton, I'd like to go with you, but I'm afraid."

"Of what?"

"Of believing all this is possible."

As much as he wanted her to help pick out their future home, he understood her concerns. "I tell you what. I'll go ahead and purchase my ideal for a farm. . .one I can afford, of course. And when we are ready to get married, you can ask for whatever revisions you'd like on the house. Is that fair?"

Katherine stared at the ground. "It's too much too soon," she whispered.

"True, and I said I wouldn't rush our relationship. All right. How about this? What if we set a time frame from when we become engaged to when we will marry. Let's say six months. . .

or a year. . .whatever time frame you feel comfortable with."

Katherine said nothing for nearly ten minutes. He prayed the entire time that she would open her heart to him.

Finally, she whispered, "I'm not being honest with you, Shelton."

eleven

Katherine braced herself for anger. Hadn't the men in her past been angry with her when she spoke her mind? Instead, Shelton was patiently waiting for her to speak. She let out a pent-up breath. "I purchased some items for my dowry." She'd carefully wrapped the horse-pattern china dishes in a bundle of gingham cloth and slid them under her bed beside the linen tablecloth and matching napkins she'd made earlier. That's where her wedding dress would go, too, when she was done with it.

Shelton's smile lit up his face. "So you *are* hoping we'll get married one day."

"Yes," she confessed, and stepped back.

He didn't move. If his heart was anything like her own, he must want to kiss her. And he would, she knew, with the slightest encouragement from her. But she didn't trust herself, so she let the chilly night air separate them.

"I'm honored, Katherine. I see it as another sign of God's healing."

"Me, too."

"What did you purchase? If you don't mind my asking."

She felt the heat of embarrassment and looked down, not wanting him to see her flushed face. "May I keep it as a surprise for you?"

"I love surprises." Shelton chuckled.

Katherine looked up and faced him. "I have another confession."

"Try me."

"I. . ." She couldn't do it. *I want to tell him I love him, Lord, but. . .* Just buying the china for her dowry had taken huge amounts of courage. "I'm sorry. I can't."

"That's all right. When you're ready to tell me, I'll be here. What's your favorite color?"

"Where did that come from?"

"I just want to get to know you better."

Katherine laughed. "You're incorrigible."

"Yes, but you love that about me. Now, what is your favorite color?"

"I love a rich, vibrant green for clothing, but my favorite color for decorating would be light purples and pinks."

"Hmm. Pink is not my favorite. But purple I could live with. In moderation."

Katherine joined him back on the rock. "How do you feel about yellow and blue?"

"If it's a mild yellow, I'm fine with it. Bright yellow, like a canary, would be too overpowering. But the yellow of a daffodil could be nice."

"I agree."

"I think we'll find we have a lot in common. But we'll also find we have a lot of differences. I like differences. I like mating my horses with ones that complement each other."

"Like Kehoe and Kate?"

"Absolutely. Kehoe is fast, has good lines, and runs a race well. Kate is light on her feet and has a fire in her eyes when pushed. I hope the twins will inherit all of those qualities from their parents."

Katherine mulled over the seriousness with which he treated his horses, especially in choosing which ones to mate for the outcome of new stock. She realized he might feel the same way about his future wife and children. "Shelton, I don't come from good stock."

"Nonsense. Look at your brother; he's an honorable man. That same quality is in you. It has to be."

"No, you don't understand. Urias got that from the MacKenneths, not from our parents. I'm not like him at all. I'm self-centered. That's why I can't commit to you. I can't trust myself."

Shelton's chest rose, then slowly deflated. She'd noticed him doing this often before he spoke. "You've given your life to help others. You sacrifice your own wants for the sake of others all the time."

"Not really. I do things for people because they give me a roof over my head and food in my belly. I love them, of course. But my first desire every day is for me. For my own place. My own freedom."

"Sounds normal to me."

She started to interrupt. He placed a finger to her lips. The gentle touch seared her heart.

"Let me explain. As much as I love my family and will do whatever I can to provide for them, my first thoughts are always for myself. It's how I respond to those thoughts that make me selfish or not. I'll wager, if you ask anyone our age—perhaps even a bit older—they would say the same thing. I don't know if our elders are beyond that. But I suspect most people are like that."

"Like what?"

"We feed, clothe, and take care of our bodies. Like the Bible tells us, no man hates his own body, but cares for it. We have to choose to put others first, before our own desires. Sure, I feel obligated to help my family. But I do it from my love for them and my love of God and my desire to serve Him. You, probably better than anyone else, understand what it means to be a servant, to obey without question. I struggle with that all the time. I have to fight off my desires and seek the Lord's desires every day."

Katherine didn't know what to say. She'd never liked the scripture verses about being God's servant, because servitude caused a bitter taste in her mouth. But did Shelton have a point? Did she respond to God in a different way because of her past? Was that a blessing? How could it be?

She gazed up at him. He waited patiently for her response. "Why do you always wait until I've processed what you're saying before speaking more to me?"

A slow smile rose on his face. "You're not going to like my answer."

Katherine braced herself.

"I've found that treating you like I would a skittish horse has been the most helpful approach."

Katherine frowned at him. "You're treating me like a horse?"

"Not exactly, but somewhat. However, I don't think putting reins on you would work." He chuckled at his own joke.

Katherine laughed with him. Then, with the intensity of a lightning bolt, a memory seared her mind. The image of her hands bound, ropes cutting into her wrists, holding her down. . . She shook her head slightly.

"Katherine, what's wrong?"

Her body trembled. She leaned into Shelton and let him envelop her in his love.

"It's all right, my dear, sweet Katherine. I'm here." His loving words massaged the mounting tension unleashed by the triggered memory.

❧

He'd done it again, said something that sent her back to that dark place. "What happened just now?"

Her body shook. "There was a time when I was tied to the bed. . ."

As Katherine poured her heart out to him, he fought back anger at what had happened to her while relishing in the joy of realizing she finally trusted him enough to expose the horrible events of her past.

"I'm so sorry you went through that."

She sniffed. "Can you still. . ."

"Love you? How can you even ask? I love you even more."

She caressed his face. "You're such an amazing man, Shelton. I do care for you, deeply."

He wanted to tease her into admitting that she loved him. But now was not the time. Her emotions were raw and exhausted. She had exposed the darkest, deepest secrets of her life to him. "I love you, Katherine."

"I want to kiss you, Shelton, but I'm afraid."

"I want to kiss you, too. But we'll wait. Give yourself some time." He took her hand. "Can I pray for you?"

She nodded.

He closed his eyes. "Father, fill Katherine with Your cleansing blood and peace. Protect her mind from the memories of the past; strengthen her to walk in Your strength and grace. Thank You for the healing You've done so far in her life. Thank You for allowing me to be a part of it. Bless us as we move forward in our relationship, and may it be founded in You." He opened his eyes and gazed at her. "God's been moving in a mighty big way today, Katherine."

"I know. It's terrifying."

"I have to admit, I would love to get my hands on those men who hurt you and do some serious bodily harm to them. But I know that's not what the Lord would have me do."

She cocked her head sideways. "Why?"

"Why would I like to harm them, or why is that not what the Lord would have me do?"

"Both, I guess." She nestled into the crook of his arm.

A whiff of her freshly washed hair caught in his nostrils, calming his raw nerves. "If I were to beat the stuffings out of them, they would have a momentary pain, but they'd heal quickly from it. While it would make me feel better, it wouldn't change them. But God's Word tells us of His vengeance against those who hurt His people. That vengeance would make your attackers realize the profound effect their actions had on you, and on others they've treated so horrendously." He still wanted to pulverize them, but he kept that piece of knowledge to himself. That was a part of him she didn't need to see.

The sound of a gun firing made them both jump.

"That was close," she said.

"Too close," he agreed. "Mac," he called out in the dark. "Urias!"

Hearing nothing, Shelton lifted his rifle and scanned the area. Nothing stirred. "I'm going to walk you to Grandma Mac's house. Stay inside. I'll come back when I know what's going on."

"All right," she whispered.

He crept slowly through the dark, conscious of every movement and sound. They reached Mrs. MacKenneth's house in ten minutes.

Back at Urias's place, he scanned the perimeter of each house and pen but found no disturbance.

Urias appeared out of the dark. "We got him!" he announced. "Mac's hanging him on a tree to make him ready for eating. Have you ever had bear meat, Shelton?"

"Can't say that I have."

"It's good, but the gristle can break your teeth."

Bear meat and gristle were the furthest thoughts from his mind. "I need to go tell Katherine everything is okay."

Urias narrowed his gaze. "Are you and she. . ."

"She's safe with me, Urias. I love her, and I'll take care of her."

"She's been through a lot. I don't want you to hurt her. If you're not serious, I suggest you back away now."

"I'm very serious, and I will be patient and wait on her. Tonight she told me everything that happened to her."

"She told you?" Urias leaned on his rifle. "She's never even told me."

"You don't want to know. I don't want to know. But it had to get out in the open between us for our relationship to go forward."

Urias stood up straight and grabbed Shelton's shoulder. "You'll give me your word you'll be honorable to her?"

"Yes, sir."

"Then you have my blessing."

"Thank you."

Urias left without saying another word.

When Shelton reached Mrs. MacKenneth's porch, he took the steps two at a time and knocked on the door. Katherine opened it right away.

"They shot the bear. Everyone is safe."

"Am I?" Her voice trembled.

"Your secret is safe with me, Katherine. And we don't need to talk about it again. . .unless you want to. I will keep praying for you and for God's healing to continue. Just remember, you are free and clean from all that has happened to you because of God's grace and the sacrifice His Son made for you and me on the cross."

"I know. It's just hard to accept sometimes."

"Yes, it is." *Someday I'll tell you about my life journey. And hopefully you'll forgive me the way God has.*

❧

Katherine read Shelton's note for the fifth time. It said he'd purchased the land he'd mentioned to her two days before.

He also wrote that he had gone back to Hazel Greene to talk with his parents, with all indications that he would be telling them about his new relationship with Katherine.

She felt betrayed. She'd opened her heart to him about her past and he had run off. Each day he was gone she tried to convince herself that he hadn't run away, that he was doing as he always said he would do—preparing a place for his parents. But old fears continued to plague her.

He'd been gone ten days before she received another letter from him.

My dear, sweet Katherine,

I love you and miss you terribly. I'm packing up my parents' house for their move to Jamestown. I had to let the last servant go, but I secured work for him with the Rawlins family over in Mount Sterling.

I'd hoped my parents would come on their own so that I'd be able to quickly return to you. However, the situation has become unbearable for Mother, and they wish to return with me. I will be back as soon as possible.

I hate to ask, but I need a favor from you. I'm wondering if you can have Urias and some of the others help clean the old farmhouse on my new property. Mac and Urias know where it is. You are familiar with my mother's tastes. If you could oversee the painting and curtains for the master suite, I'd appreciate it. I know I'm asking a lot from you, but you're the only one I trust to do right for them.

Yours forever,
Shelton

Katherine read the letter three times before running to Urias and asking him to take her to Shelton's new house.

She and Urias's family did a thorough inspection of the

place. Urias found some structural issues that required immediate attention.

The farmhouse was in such disrepair Katherine wondered if Shelton had ever seen it in the daylight. For the next three days, the MacKenneths, the O'Learys, and other neighbors cleaned, painted, and fixed the interior of the house. Urias said they'd have to wait to paint the exterior until spring. Katherine made curtains for the master bedroom, living room, dining area, and kitchen. Prudence washed the kitchen, scrubbing through layers of soot until she could see the yellowed wood of the knotty pine cabinets and the cast iron of the stove gleamed black. Pamela scrubbed the walls and floors. The men repaired trim, doors, windows, and a serious problem with the center beam of the foundation. Then they cleared the drive from the road to the house.

Katherine wondered why Shelton had purchased this place. Until she saw the view from the second-story master bedroom window. Spread out before her was a clear view of the Cumberland River at one of its widest points. It was so expansive she could have mistaken it for a lake.

She peeled off the bedroom's wallpaper and applied a fresh coat of paint. If the bed were positioned against the wall opposite the window, one could look out over the river. She'd love to wake up to that view every morning. But Shelton had said this room was for his parents. He was giving them the best view in the house. Katherine remembered Shelton's determination to honor them. He certainly was doing it now. If she and Shelton were to marry, she would have to honor them as well. She wondered if she could do it.

From her own savings, Katherine had purchased fabric for the curtains and accent pillows for the bed. There was enough to reupholster the chair and ottoman. . .if Mrs. Greene would like.

At the end of the first week, the house seemed habitable. Everyone went back to their daily responsibilities. . .except Katherine. She wanted to make the house as fit for Shelton and his parents as she could.

In her heart she knew that, even if the Greens could never see her as anything other than a bondservant, she should love them in the same way Shelton did. From everything he'd said, that would at times be a choice, not a feeling.

She tried not to think about what it would be like to have the Greens living so close. There were plenty of other issues to deal with. Perhaps the fact that the house was in such disrepair was a good thing. It made her concentrate on work rather than on foolish meandering through the past.

She had no idea what items of furniture his parents would be able to bring along. Would Shelton restrict them to a single wagon load?

Katherine stood on a stool to hang the last of the curtains in the front sitting room. She spotted Shelton with a wagon full of furniture coming toward the house. He was alone.

She jumped off the stool, raced out of the house, and ran across the field to greet him. "Shelton!" she called, waving as she ran.

He pulled up a few yards from the house and stared at her. "Katherine, you're a sight for sore eyes." He nodded at the house. "Please don't tell me you're still working on the place."

"You don't know the half of it."

"I'm afraid I do." He hopped to the ground and dusted off his trousers.

"Where are your parents?"

"I dropped them off at Prudence's house so I could unload some of their furniture first. Mac told me how bad the house was. I'm sorry. If I'd known it was that bad, I wouldn't have asked you to help fix it up."

"Nonsense. I saw the view from the master bedroom. I would have wanted the house, too."

Shelton's blue eyes danced with merriment. He brushed away a curl that dangled over her right eye. "I've missed you so much."

"I've missed you, too."

She reached for his hand. "Come, let me show you what we've done."

He held her hand and gave it a quick squeeze.

twelve

Shelton couldn't believe the transformation of the house. He held Katherine's hand and caressed the top of it with his thumb as they looked over the river from the master bedroom. The sun sparkled on the little ripples of water. It was a splendid sight, even more enchanting than when he viewed it a few weeks ago.

"Katherine, this room is marvelous. I can't believe you did all this. Mother will be thrilled."

"I saved some fabric to cover her chair and ottoman. Were you able to bring them?"

"I did. We have two wagons full of furniture and other belongings. Father drove one wagon, and I drove the other." *And hidden deep in my wagon is the family heirloom I hope to give you one day.* He prayed the precious family heirloom, a china vase, hadn't broken during the trip.

"Was it difficult for them to leave their home?"

"It was horrible. Apparently news traveled fast about Father's financial situation, and the reason for it. Mother said none of her friends would even speak with her."

"I'm so sorry."

"Father has lost his will to go on. I don't know how to reach him. I'm praying this new house will be just what he needs to get back on his feet."

"I hope so."

"I managed to sell the house rather than have the bank acquire it. That produced some much-needed funds. And we earned a profit from the coal mines. I sold that land but retained the mineral rights, so we'll receive a percentage of the profit—if the mine makes a profit. It will give my parents a small income each year."

"You're a wise businessman, Shelton. I'm so proud of you."

He beamed at her praise. "So, what do you think of the place?"

"I haven't looked over the land, but the house will be wonderful once it's done. Urias said we have to wait until spring to paint the exterior."

"I hope my parents come visit the place in the dark first. Then they'll see the exterior after they've seen what everyone has done on the inside. Still, it won't be like their old home. I hope they can adjust to it."

She nodded.

"Do you think you can adjust to them?"

Her smooth forehead crinkled. "I've tried to honor your parents the way you do, simply for being your parents. But it's hard."

"I'm just pleased that you've tried. You're an incredible woman, Katherine. I can't believe you did all this for them. Urias and Prudence told me you did all the work in the master suite. I wish this room was ours."

A slight smile creased her lips. "I do, too. But they deserve a room like this for their sanctuary."

"And you've made it into one. Thank you."

"Come." She took him by the hand. "Let me show you your room."

"My room?"

"Well, the room I thought you might enjoy as yours."

"Lead on." He marveled at the softness of her hand. Soft but sturdy, hard-working hands, unlike his own. Then again, he reflected, his hands were not the same as when he left home months ago.

She gripped his fingers a bit more tightly as she led him inside the room.

She had decorated it in masculine earth tones. A painting of a horse hung on the wall. She had placed a rustic bouquet of dried autumn flowers on the nightstand. A dark green spread draped over the bed.

"Where did you get this?"

"I splurged and purchased the fabric. It's only a cover. I didn't have time to make an actual quilt, but I thought this would do."

"It's beautiful. Thank you."

"You're welcome."

"Katherine, it's too much. Let me pay you for your time."

She stiffened and released his hand.

"I'm sorry. I didn't mean to offend you. It's just that I know you've been saving for—"

She placed a finger to his lips. In spite of his firm resolve, he gave in to the powerful desire and gave her finger a light kiss.

Her breathing became ragged. "Shelton, I. . .I. . ." She pulled away.

"I'm sorry. I promise not to kiss you again until you ask me to."

"You don't understand. I want to so much, I ache. But I don't think. . .I mean. . ."

"You're worried you'll cross the line from a chaste kiss to the kind of passionate kiss reserved for marriage?"

"Yes."

"I understand, and I respect that. I'll wait until you're ready. Until we're both ready."

"I feel horrible about this. I know what God designed. It's just that. . ."

"Shh." He placed his finger to her lips. "It's all right. I know.

And God will give us the strength to deal with the wait."

"I don't deserve you." Katherine turned away from him and held her sides.

"No, Katherine, you deserve better than me. But I'm confident of God's desire for us to become one someday. We will get past this."

He glanced around the room one more time. "Let's unpack before my parents arrive."

"Too late," Hiram Greene announced from the hallway. "Which room is ours?"

Shelton walked out to the hallway. "That one." He pointed to the doorway on the opposite end of the hall.

Hiram nodded and bent to pick up a heavy-looking wood crate. Shelton helped him carry it into the master suite.

"Oh, my," Elizabeth Greene crooned as she entered the room. "Shelton, this is beautiful."

"You can thank Katherine for that."

"You mean Kate?"

"She prefers to be called Katherine, Mother."

"I didn't know that. I'll try to remember. Where is she?"

"I'm right here, ma'am." She hovered in the doorway, her face pale.

"You did an exquisite job on the master bedroom. But won't you and Shelton want this room for yourselves?"

Katherine glanced at Shelton.

He shrugged. "I told them we hoped to get married in the future."

"Oh." Katherine cleared her throat. "Shelton and I felt this room would be a good place for the two of you. There's a great view of the river."

"Are you sure, son?" Hiram asked.

"Yes, sir. This is your room. Katherine did everything you see here."

"Thank you," he mumbled.

Shelton's stomach tightened as his father looked at the floor.

"There are fresh linens and pillows in the closet," Katherine said. "When the men get your bed put together, I'll be happy to make it up for you."

Elizabeth Greene smiled. "Nonsense, you've done enough."

❧

Katherine didn't know what to think. These people were a faded image of who they once were. Her heart went out to them in a way she'd never dreamed possible. She took Shelton's hand. "Come and help me."

He followed her down the stairs and out the door.

"Shelton, what's happened to them?"

"This transition has been very hard on them."

"They're definitely not the same people."

"No, they're not. But I'm worried. Father doesn't seem to have much of a will to live. I know he disapproves of our union, but he doesn't have the strength to fight me on it. If he starts feeling better soon, I imagine we'll exchange a few words on the subject."

Katherine let out a pent-up gasp of air. "I'll be praying for him." A part of her liked that Mr. Greene was not acting boisterous and arguing. But another part understood that something was wrong.

"Hopefully one day he'll regain his strength *and* approve of our marriage."

Katherine chuckled. "Did anyone ever tell you you're an optimist?"

"Yes. My father. You two are quite alike sometimes."

Katherine bristled at the comparison, but then realized that maybe Shelton was right. She had very strong opinions, although most people didn't know it. If anyone did, it was Shelton.

He pointed out the living room window. "Here come Urias and Mac with the rest of the furniture."

Katherine pretty much stayed out of the way while the men moved in the various pieces. So many treasured items from the house in Hazel Greene had not been packed. Katherine hated to think about all that the Greens had lost. Items she had spent hours dusting, cleaning, arranging. Possessions that set their home apart from others in the area. She particularly remembered the old china vase that had belonged to Hiram's great-grandfather, who used to captain ships around the world. Katherine wondered who now owned all those things, did they cherish them as much as Mrs. Greene once had?

It didn't matter. Now was the time to rebuild. With God's help, and with Shelton's, perhaps one day the Greens would live a gay life again.

❧

Katherine spent the next day helping Grandma Mac. Her house had been neglected since Katherine had taken on the project of fixing up Shelton's home.

"It's such a shame." Grandma Mac rocked back and forth in her rocker. "But at least the Greens have their health, and they're back with family. With God's grace, they'll get through this transition in their lives."

"I hope so."

"I hear you did some mighty fancy work in that house. Tell me about it."

Katherine went into great detail about all the remodeling and sewing she'd done for the place.

"My, my. Have you been able to fill your orders for Mr. Hastings as well?"

"Not yet. I have to make one more shirt tonight. Then I can take everything in tomorrow morning. I have to purchase more needles with my next order. The ones I've been using are getting worn down."

"I don't doubt it. Now, tell me, have you and Shelton kissed yet?"

"You're far too preoccupied with other people's romances."

"True. But I sense you and Shelton have grown closer."

"Yes, we have. But no kisses yet. Although he did kiss my finger. Does that count?"

Grandma Mac laughed out loud. "It's a start. I think that boy has spent too much time with his horses."

Katherine chuckled. *I wonder if she knows how very much I wanted to kiss him.*

❧

Shelton spent the first month after his parents' arrival getting the new barn ready for Kehoe and Kate. Katherine helped build a fence for the corral, but other than that, they spent precious little time with each other. He ached to talk with her. While he was certain she wanted to be with him, he had to help his parents adjust to their new living environment.

Tonight would be different. He planned to spend the evening with Katherine and Grandma Mac.

Shelton cleaned up from his work, dressed in his Sunday morning trousers, and put on a crisp white shirt with a black bow tie. He opted to leave the suit coat at home and wear instead the warmer leather jacket Prudence and Urias had given him. The first snowfall of the year had provided a light dusting on the ground. The air would be crisp come evening.

As he ran a comb through his unruly hair, he thought about the twins. They were doing well, their bushy winter coats growing in nicely. He'd purchased a half dozen chickens and a piglet to raise over the winter. Urias and Mac had provided fresh meat and winter vegetables for the new household.

His father seemed to gain strength every day, but he still

lacked focus and purpose. His mother was blissfully happy with her grandchildren nearby. Katherine's infrequent appearances to his home concerned him. She told him on many occasions she had no purpose being there, and she had chores and obligations elsewhere. He prayed that was true, but in his heart he knew she was avoiding his parents. This, like everything else, would take time.

"My, you're looking handsome this afternoon," his mother said when he joined her in the living room.

"Thank you."

"How's Kate?"

"Katherine," he corrected.

"Forgive me. She answered to Kate for so many years, it's hard to remember."

Didn't she realize that was the reason Katherine preferred her proper name?

"Do you know where your father is?"

"He said he was going to Creelsboro today to look for work."

"Oh, that's right. Well, I'm visiting with Prudence and the children this evening. We're going to make Christmas gifts after the children go to bed."

"Would you like me to pick you up after my dinner with Katherine and Mrs. MacKenneth?"

"That would be lovely, dear. Thank you."

Shelton bid his mother good-bye and headed off to Mrs. MacKenneth's. He'd been contemplating for days what to get Katherine for Christmas. He wanted just the right gift, but kept coming up blank.

He arrived fifteen minutes early and settled Kehoe in the barn for the evening.

"Hi there, handsome." Katherine's green eyes sparkled.

Shelton's heart pounded. "Hi, beautiful. You look real good."

A rich evergreen dress cascaded down her body, accenting her feminine form. A white lace collar framed her glorious face.

"Grandma Mac sent me out to fetch you. Frankly, the old woman is a matchmaker above all matchmakers. But I like having the chance to be alone with you for a few moments."

Shelton cherished her acknowledgment. How long had it taken her to come to that point? *Thank You, Lord.* "I'm glad we have a few minutes alone, too."

She reached out and he took her hand. She pulled him closer. "Shelton," she whispered, "I want to kiss you."

He fought off the desire to swoop her up in his arms and kiss her with all the passion he had for her. "Are you sure?"

"Yes. But we must promise each other not to let our desires run away from our self-control."

"I promise." He gently caressed her face. His fingers tingled from the closeness.

She closed her eyes.

He brushed her lips with his thumb. "You're sure?" he asked in a whisper.

Her eyes sprung open. "If you don't kiss me now, I won't be able to kiss you for a very long time."

He could see the fire of passion in her eyes. *Lord, give me strength.* He moved in slowly. "I love you, Katherine." He placed a slow, soft kiss on her lips. She relaxed and returned the kiss. Her hands ruffled through his hair.

Shelton pulled back and counted to ten in an attempt to gain self-control. It wasn't working.

Katherine leaned into him. Shelton kissed her neck. "I have to stop, Katherine."

She pulled away, her eyes wide and glistening.

He held her in a gentle embrace. "I will always cherish our first kiss."

Her lips curled upward. "Me, too."

Shelton chuckled and stepped out of the embrace. "You're right. We have to keep the promise not to give in to our desires."

"That will be difficult."

She has no idea. Or perhaps she did. Either way, he knew that her kiss sent a spark of desire through him that was so strong it would take all of his willpower to remain an honorable man.

And he still hadn't told her about his past yet.

thirteen

Two weeks and ten kisses later, Katherine felt like she could handle her emotions when she was with Shelton. He'd been the strong one, and she was grateful for it.

On her way into Creelsboro, she couldn't stop thinking about him. Day and night, he was always on her mind. Grandma Mac had told her the best way to handle those kinds of thoughts were to turn them into prayers for Shelton, for the Lord to bless him and strengthen him. She'd prayed the entire two hours to Creelsboro.

"Good morning, Mr. Hastings." The scent of oiled leather filled the store. Every time Katherine entered this place it had a different smell. It all depended on what new merchandise had come in.

"Good morning, Miss O'Leary. Have you got my order?"

"Yes, sir. I also made a couple of dolls. With Christmas coming, I thought you might be able to sell them."

"I'm sure I can. But I probably won't be needin' any more clothing until spring. There aren't many folks traveling west this time of year."

"I understand."

"I'll send word to you once I need more." He scribbled a few notations in his ledger book, then walked to the cash register. "Have you and Shelton set a date yet?"

"Not yet. He wants his parents to settle in first."

The cash drawer opened and he pulled out a piece of paper. "Would you give this to Shelton?" The store owner handed her a slip of paper. "His father's been charging, and he's run up quite a bill."

Katherine clamped her mouth shut. Hiram didn't have a job and was living off his son's income. *What could he be purchasing?* It wasn't her place to ask. "I'll be happy to." She took the paper and slipped it into her purse.

She glanced over the housewares section of the store. "Where's the tea set?"

"Sold it last week."

Katherine's heart sank. She'd been saving for a month to purchase the service. It was a full set, with teapot, sugar, creamer, and a silver serving tray, rare in these parts.

"Forgive me, Katherine. I didn't realize you wanted it."

"That's all right. I'll just get some more linen to make a tablecloth and matching napkins for Prudence's Christmas present." She had plenty of time to sew now that she'd finished making her wedding dress. The task had seemed presumptuous since they weren't officially engaged yet. But Shelton had promised they would marry one day, and she believed him.

She moved to the leather works section. Shelton would love a new bit and brace for Kehoe. "How much are these?"

They settled on a fair price and she put off the linens for another time. Next, she purchased some flannel to make undergarments for the family for Christmas. It was a practical gift; she knew how thin those undergarments would get before a new set was made.

Her money spent, she loaded her packs and headed for her horse.

A ruckus down the street caught her attention. Katherine looked over her shoulder and saw a drunk being kicked out of the saloon. She didn't see such a sight often, but knew all too well the evils of drink.

The drunk landed face down in the mud of the street.

"And stay out!" she heard the barkeeper yell. Inside, a roar of laughter followed.

Katherine shook her head and prayed the man's family could help him.

She mounted her horse. The way home went past the saloon. When she passed the drunk, he lifted himself out of the mud.

"Oh no."

❧

Shelton handed his Christmas gift for Katherine to his mother, asking her to polish it to perfection. He'd found the silver tea tray in the mercantile, and Mr. Hastings had told him that Katherine had her eye on it for weeks. The store owner had conducted a healthy bartering session. Finally Shelton agreed to sell him some of his grain harvest next year, provided he had a surplus. Not being a farmer, he had no idea how well his crops would grow.

He sat at the kitchen table while his mother examined the silver set. "This is very nice, Shelton. Katherine will love it."

"I hope so." Shelton shifted in his seat, then mustered up the most casual voice he could. "Have you seen Father?"

"Not since this morning. He said he had some business in town."

This was getting to be a habit. His father had been going to Creelsboro every day for weeks, but he hadn't come back with a job or any legitimate-sounding explanation of what he'd been doing there. One time Shelton smelled alcohol on his father's breath, but Hiram passed it off as having brushed up against a man with an open flask. Back in Hazel Greene his father would have an occasional drink. But as far as Shelton knew, he drank in moderation and only during social visits.

Concerned that his father might be gambling again, he rode Kehoe to Creelsboro.

Near town, he saw a horse with a sickly looking rider on it. A woman walked beside the horse. With a start, he recognized her face. "Katherine?"

"Shelton! Thank God you're here."

He got a good look at the man bent over the saddle horn. "Father?"

"He was kicked out of the saloon," Katherine explained. "I'm afraid he's not doing well."

Shelton dismounted. He came up beside Katherine's horse and took the reigns. "Father, are you all right?"

Hiram leaned off the other side of the horse and vomited.

"Do you know what happened?" he asked Katherine.

"His breath reeks of liquor. But my mother didn't get this sick when she drank. Is he used to alcohol?"

"I've never known him to be a heavy drinker."

"Don't be talkin' 'bout me as if I wasn't here," Hiram scolded, his words slurred.

"What happened, Father?"

"I got drunk."

Shelton shared a look of frustration with Katherine.

"You still plannin' on marryin' that tramp?" Hiram sneered.

"You will not speak of Katherine that way."

"I ain't talkin' 'bout her. I mean the other one." Hiram started to slide off the saddle.

Shelton caught his father and looked at Katherine, who was staring back at him, a huge question in her green eyes. "Later," he told her.

He could see her nostrils flare.

"Ride Kehoe to my house and tell Mother I'll be back as soon as I can."

She nodded, mounted his horse, and left without saying a word.

He knew he should have told her sooner. Now his father

had spilled his past in a drunken stupor. He walked beside the horse, steadying Hiram on the saddle.

After a couple of hours, his father's words were less slurred, and he began to make sense.

"What happened, Dad?"

"I can't say."

Shelton balled his fists and slowly released them. "Have you been gambling again?"

Hiram nodded.

"Wonderful. I move you to a new place to make a clean start, and this is the thanks I get? How many people do you owe now?"

"I'll take care of my affairs, son. You can mind your own business."

"You can't take care of anything. How are you planning to pay your debts?"

Hiram coughed, then vomited again.

"Mother's going to love seeing you like this," Shelton quipped.

"Don't tell her."

"There's no way to keep this from her."

"I beg you, please don't tell your mother. She'll leave me for sure. You don't know how bad things were in Hazel Greene. How bad they still are between us. She hardly speaks to me. Please, you can't tell her."

"Dad, it isn't a question of my telling her. You need to be honest with your wife. About your insecurities, your failures, everything."

"Like you've been with that wench." Hiram spat.

"Don't you ever speak about her like that again. Or so help me, I'll. . ."

"You ain't got the guts."

Shelton curled his fingers into a fist.

"Go ahead, hit me. I dare you."

Shelton relaxed his hand. "No. I won't hit a man when he's down. You have a decision to make, Dad. Either you change or I'm kicking you out of my house."

"You can't do that!"

"Can't I? You're living on my land, Dad. My property. You have nothing left."

"You can't treat me like a child. I'm your father." Hiram slurred.

"You have three days to make your decision, Dad."

They traveled the rest of the way in silence.

Shelton helped his father down from the horse. Hiram wobbled a couple of steps, then fell to the ground.

"Shelton!" his mother shrieked as she ran to them from the porch. "What happened?"

"He has a serious problem, Mom. And it goes beyond gambling. I gave him three days to make a decision to change. If he doesn't, I'm kicking him out. You can stay if you want."

Shelton mounted Katherine's horse and headed to Grandma Mac's house.

❧

Katherine paced in her room. Hiram Greene's comment made her question everything Shelton had ever said to her. Apparently, he wanted to marry someone else. Katherine held her sides and tried to brace herself for the truth.

Was Hiram confused because he was drunk? Did she look so different that he was thinking of her in the past? Maybe that was it.

She wouldn't know until she spoke with Shelton. She didn't want to confront the situation, but knew she had to.

She went to the kitchen to prepare for the evening meal. She found Grandma Mac there, putting on her heavy winter coat.

"I'll be spending the evening with Mac and Pamela," the older woman said. "Nash Jr. is coming to fetch me." Nash Jr. was the oldest of Pamela and Mac's children. At nine years of age, he was so proud to be old enough to drive the wagon by himself, he offered rides to anyone who wanted them.

Katherine took down a couple of the canned foods Grandma Mac had prepared earlier in the year. Her hand trembled and one of the jars crashed to the counter.

"Are you all right, dear?"

"I'm fine."

Grandma Mac snickered. "If you're fine, I'd hate to see what wonderful is like."

"I'll be okay. I just have to calm down."

"From what?"

Nash Jr. knocked on the door and came right in. "Hi, Grandma, I'm here." He gave Katherine a slight bow. "Evenin', Miss O'Leary."

"Evenin', Master Nash." Katherine tilted her head slightly to the side and smiled. "Have a good night tonight. And don't beat your Grandma too badly in checkers."

Nash Jr. chuckled. "Grandma doesn't allow me to win anymore. I have to win on my own now."

"You're too smart," Grandma Mac chimed in. "You win about half the time. Next year I won't be able to play with you at all."

Grandma Mac and Nash said their good-byes and left her alone. She had craved solitude for so long, yet now that she had it, she wasn't sure she liked it. She'd prefer to have someone in the house with her. It seemed more comfortable. "What's wrong with me, Lord? I beg for my own place, and now I can't stand being alone. Will I ever be normal?"

All in good time, a gentle whisper spoke inside her head.

She wondered how Shelton was dealing with his father.

Will there ever come a day when his parents aren't his first priority? When I am?

The door rattled in its jamb as a knock resounded through the house.

"Who is it?"

"Shelton. May I come in?"

She opened the door. He looked weary, beaten.

He stomped the dirt off his boots and came inside. "I'm sorry you found my father in such a state."

"I'm glad I was there to take him home. Did he tell you what happened?"

"Not in words, but I'm certain he was gambling. Probably lost a lot of money he didn't have and then drank too much." Shelton took off his coat and sat on the sofa.

Katherine sat across from him in the rocking chair.

"Katherine, we need to talk about what my father said."

She began to shake. She didn't want to believe it was true. She couldn't speak, so she gave a simple nod for him to continue.

He swallowed. "I've tried to tell you this a few times, but never found the right opportunity. Forgive me."

She nodded again.

"When my father sent me away at sixteen, I was very angry. While I was away from home, I took advantage of a young lady. She conceived."

Katherine squeezed her eyes closed. *No, this can't be. Not Shelton. He's a gentleman.*

"Father offered her family money to go away. They were so upset, they refused to listen to him or me. I was banned from ever seeing her again."

Bile rose in her throat. Her head was telling her this wasn't the man she wanted to marry. Her heart felt like it was tearing apart.

"A while later, I heard she lost the baby."

Tears edged her eyelids.

"I offered to marry her, but her family refused. So I snuck into her house one night, planning to take her to a preacher. The family found me and beat me. Someone pulled a knife—" He pulled up his shirt and pointed to a large scar under his right arm.

Her heart tightened. She wanted to reach out and touch him. She laced her fingers together, keeping her hands folded in her lap.

"Why didn't you tell me about this sooner?"

"I tried to. But I was afraid if you knew I'd been less than honorable in the past, you wouldn't trust me."

"You're right. I wouldn't have trusted you." Sadness and anger swirled in her mind. This had to be a bad dream. "Did you love her?"

"No. That's even more shameful. I used her. I'm not worthy of your love, Katherine. I've told you that before, but I don't think you believed me. Now you know."

"What else have you not told me?" She rocked back to get a better look at his face.

"Nothing. Well, I'm sure there are moments when I must have done other wrong things, but nothing so serious."

After all this time thinking he was so perfect, hearing this about him sent myriad emotions coursing through her heart, all vying for supremacy. Anger quickly won. "I felt so dirty compared to you."

Shelton hung his head. "I know. I'm sorry. You were innocent of what happened to you. I was the guilty person. But I also know of God's redemptive power. He has forgiven me for my actions." Shelton knelt before her. "Can you?"

She closed her eyes. Could she forgive him? Could she trust him? *If he lied about this. . . Well, he didn't actually lie, he just omitted this part of his past. But can I believe that there isn't more to tell?* "I don't know."

Shelton's hands shook. He stood, stared at her for a moment, then left the room in silence.

Katherine's heart broke and she wept. The man she loved was not the man she thought he was.

fourteen

Shelton split more logs than he had use for. Katherine had not spoken to him for three days. Today was the deadline for his father to decide if he was going to change his ways or pack his bags. Shelton found himself not caring what his father decided. Nothing mattered if Katherine wasn't going to be a part of his life.

"Shelton?" his mother called from the back door of the kitchen.

"Be right there." He swung the axe into the block and left it there. He grabbed his coat and walked back to the house.

Inside he found his mother and father sitting at the table. Parson Kincaid sat next to them. "Parson." Shelton extended his hand. "What can I do for you?"

"I'm here at your parents' request."

Shelton took a seat.

"Shel," his mother said, "your father and I want to stay."

Shelton stared at his dad. "He knows my conditions."

Hiram kept his gaze away from Shelton.

"That's why I'm here," Parson Kincaid offered. "Your father has told me he is willing to change. But he didn't think you'd believe him."

"He has a tongue. He can speak for himself." Shelton continued to stare at his father.

"And who made you lord and master?" Hiram growled. Squinting his right eye, he glared at Shelton. "You're not perfect yourself."

"And thanks to you, Katherine knows all about it. I was

going to tell her at the right opportunity. She didn't deserve to hear it from a drunk."

"What on earth are you two talking about?" his mother cried.

Shelton inhaled deeply and counted to ten before exhaling. "I'm sorry, Mother. But when I was sixteen and Father sent me away, I took advantage of a young lady. Father tried to pay the family off. They didn't appreciate the offer. They refused to even let me talk with her and wanted me to have nothing to do with the baby."

Elizabeth Greene's eyes widened. "I have a grandchild I don't know about?" she whispered.

"No. I received word that she lost the baby. I've repented and God has been gracious to me ever since."

"And your pious attitude has been destroying this family," Hiram accused.

"Hiram," the parson said, "do you really blame Shelton for your gambling problem?"

Hiram coughed. "No."

"But you don't like your son telling you what to do, right?"

"Precisely."

"Parson," Shelton said, "I've heard his vows to change before. I've been dealing with this problem for nearly a year now. I don't trust his word."

The parson turned toward Hiram. "What do you have to say about this?"

He pushed the chair back and stood. "I'll be moved out in an hour."

"Hiram," Elizabeth cried. She turned to her son and the parson. "Could you give us some privacy, please?"

They left the room and stood out on the porch.

"You're forcing your father to make some hard choices," Parson Kincaid said.

"I know. But I don't think he'll change if I keep providing for him and bailing him out of all the jams he gets into."

"You mean like he did for you when you were younger?"

Shelton thought back on that time. His father had tried to help. It wasn't the right kind of help, but at least he did try. "Every time he tried to step in, he made the wrong choice. Money doesn't solve all our problems. It's the heart that matters."

"And has your heart hardened toward your father?"

"No, Parson. I still love him. That's why it hurts so much to see him like this."

"Has anyone threatened to have him arrested for his debts?" Parson Kincaid asked.

Shelton sat on the rail. "Not here. But back in Hazel Greene he would have gone to jail if not for me. I took care of things for him. But I see now that didn't really help. Perhaps I made things worse for him. I don't know. I just know that I'm not doing him any favors by letting him live here for free."

"Then may I suggest another alternative?"

"What do you have in mind, Parson?"

❧

Katherine felt miserable. She couldn't imagine life without Shelton. But now she knew she couldn't trust him. In her mind she'd gone over what Shelton said again and again, but couldn't get away from the fact that he should have told her sooner. His confession now led her to be suspicious of him. If she hadn't heard the words of his father, would he have ever told her?

"Lord, this is nonsense," she moaned.

"You got that right." Grandma Mac had a way of sneaking up on a person. "Tell me, child, what happened the other night?"

Katherine took in a shaky breath. "Shelton has a past."

"Don't we all?" Grandma Mac sat down on a nearby rocking chair.

Katherine continued to press the pleats of the outfit she'd made for Elizabeth Katherine for Christmas. "Hiram Greene is a beast."

"What did he do?"

"He's a horrible drunk."

"That isn't so extreme."

Katherine put down the iron and took the little dress off the board. She folded it neatly and set it aside. She wasn't nearly as mad at Hiram Greene as she was with Shelton. "Shelton had an. . . indiscretion."

"What did he do? When?"

"When he was sixteen."

"I see. And that makes you feel, what? Foolish because you felt so sinful compared to him?"

"Yes." Foolish. Betrayed. Katherine had so many emotions swimming around in her heart she couldn't trust her own thoughts, much less her words or actions.

"Tell me, my dear, before you became comfortable with Shelton, didn't you think of yourself as being more sinful than most people?"

"Well, yes."

"So Shelton becoming a part of your life had nothing to do with how you felt about yourself."

"His presence made it worse. . .at first."

"Did it? Or did it simply force you to deal with unresolved hurts, pains, and matters of trust between you and the Lord?"

Katherine thought for a moment. She had to admit, her relationship with Shelton had helped bring her to a place of genuine healing.

"It seems to me that you've been unable to trust for a long time. You've held on to the bondage of past sins rather than go through the painful process of letting go and letting God free you. When Shelton came along, you forced yourself to face those painful memories and give them over to the Lord once and for all. Am I right?"

Katherine groaned. Did Grandma Mac have an ear horn against the door every time she poured her heart out to the Lord? "I don't like it when you're right."

Grandma Mac gave a hearty laugh. "You mean when God's right. Child, I'm an old woman. I've seen a lot of things in my life. Age and experience have given me a perspective that's more straightforward than I had when I was younger. Oh, I made mistakes when I was young, and I've had to battle with my emotions until I completely surrendered them to the Lord. After I did, I wondered why I took so long to do it. Foolish pride, I guess. Only the good Lord knows. But our God is a God of action and change. He's forever moving, and He wants us to move forward in our lives. You've broken through the bondage of the past. The question is, are you going to forgive and move forward into the relationship God has designed for you?"

Had God really designed Shelton for her? Were they meant to have a life together? A couple of weeks ago she wouldn't have questioned it. Did it really matter that Shelton did something he was ashamed of, that he repented of? "You don't mince words, do you?"

"I'm glad it hurts, dear. Giving up our ability to retreat and lick our wounds always hurts. We must allow God to dig deeper and help us rid ourselves of all the memories that will fester and become ugly unless the Lord lances our wounds. Think about it, pray about it. But most important, do what is right and holy in God's eyes. . .not yours, mine, Hiram's, or Shelton's."

She didn't want to admit it, but Grandma Mac made sense. If she gave in to all her anger and embarrassment, she would be right back where she'd started.

Grandma Mac stood and patted her shoulder. Then she shuffled out of the room without saying another word.

Katherine went back to ironing her Christmas presents. Working with her hands seemed better than dealing with the words Grandma Mac had just spoken. But she couldn't stop thinking about them. She replayed the conversation over and over. Then she remembered Shelton saying that one day he would tell her about his past and how unworthy he was. *He had said that.* He wasn't trying to hide this from her.

"Dear Lord, can Shelton and I have the kind of relationship you designed for a man and woman? Can we ever have the completeness that will make us one? Or will our pasts always get in the way?"

❧

"Katherine, I need to speak with you," Shelton called from outside her bedroom door. He'd waited for three days to talk to her. Now, after the recent visit from Parson Kincaid, he had no choice. "Please, Katherine. Something has come up."

"I'll be right there." He heard her scurrying about in her room.

Shelton stepped back and waited. When she peeked out the doorway, he felt thrilled to see her crown of red curls. "Do you have a minute?"

She looked into her room, then back at him. "Sure. Wait for me in the sitting room." She closed the door.

Shelton nearly skipped toward the sitting room. *At least she didn't throw something at me.* He grinned. He sat on the sofa, then jumped up and paced before the fireplace.

Katherine came in with her hair straightened.

"Katherine, I'm so sorry."

"Shh. I'm sorry. I overreacted."

"I don't think so. One day soon we'll discuss what happened

in greater detail, but right now I want to speak with you about something Parson Kincaid just suggested."

She sat on the sofa. "All right."

"I know we talked about waiting to get married until we were ready, but Parson Kincaid thinks we might want to change those plans."

"Why?"

"He thinks I was being less than generous to give my father only three days to make a decision about how he was going to live his life. But he had an alternative."

Shelton sat beside her. "The parson believes that if we marry now, we may be able to help Father stop his gambling habit. It would take a long time and a lot of work. We'd have to watch over him constantly and not let him out of our sight."

"And what does that have to do with our getting married?"

"Parson Kincaid knows we're planning on getting married eventually anyway. His suggestion is that we do it sooner rather than later. Between the two of us, we can keep a better eye on him. And we could find strength in each other."

"But Parson Kincaid doesn't know about my past. He doesn't know how difficult the adjustment will be, especially in our first year together. I think adding your parents' issues and your father's gambling habits into the mix would be foolhardy."

Shelton leaned back in the sofa. "You're right, he doesn't know about you. But he knows about me."

"How?"

"My father, in his anger, blurted it out in front of my mother and the parson."

She took his hand.

"Father's blaming me for his problems."

"Then he's not ready to stop gambling."

"No, he isn't. So he's going to have to move out of my house.

Mother insists on going with him."

"Does she know how bad your father's problem is?"

"Yes. That's what perplexes me. Why does she want to stay with him?"

Katherine smiled. "Because she loves him."

"Well, there is that." Shelton's shoulders slumped. "What should I do?"

"They're not children. You can't order them about. You have to let them make their own choices—right or wrong."

"But he'll gamble again."

"No doubt. But isn't there a church right down the street from the saloon?"

"Yes."

"Maybe if your parents have nowhere to go and no one to fall back on, they'll make the right choice."

"I still don't like it."

"I don't either. But maybe that's what it's going to take. We're not so far from town that we can't keep tabs on them."

Katherine stuffed her hands in her pockets to warm them. She felt the piece of paper Mr. Hastings had given her. "Oh, I almost forgot. Mr. Hastings gave this to me the day I found your father. Apparently he's been charging at the store."

Shelton took the crumpled piece of paper and read. "My father charged fifty dollars' worth of merchandize to my account."

"Oh, my. I think before they move into town, you should advise the businessmen that you are not responsible for your father's debts."

"You're a wise woman, Katherine."

"I've been around a lot of gamblers."

He placed his hands on her shoulders. "Would you go to my house and tell my parents they can stay for another night? I want to go into town and talk with the business owners right away. If I go speak with my parents now, I know I'm just going to blow up at Father. I need to know how far he's put me in debt before I speak with them. Ask them to stay for one more night. I'll see them in the morning."

"All right."

Shelton took her hands into his. "Katherine, will you still marry me?"

"Is that a proposal?" she asked.

"I just want to know if you're ready."

"Not quite yet, but I'm getting there. With you in my life, I don't care what other nonsense I have to deal with. I just want you by my side."

He smiled.

"Kiss me before I say something foolish," she encouraged.

And he did.

fifteen

Katherine prayed the entire trip from Grandma Mac's house to Shelton's. She had no idea what she would find when she arrived, or how Hiram Greene would respond to her.

"Hello," she called out as she entered the front door. "Is anyone home?"

Elizabeth Greene came from the front parlor, her eyes puffy and red.

"Mrs. Greene, Shelton asked me to come over and let you know that you can stay for one more night."

"We'll not be taking any more charity from him," Hiram gruffed as he entered the room. "As soon as the boy tells us which wagon is ours, we'll be on our way."

"Shelton will be back late this evening. That's why he suggested you leave tomorrow."

Hiram turned to face his wife. "Let's just take one, Elizabeth. I can't stand to be in this house another minute."

Before she could answer, Katherine said, "I'm sorry you feel that way, Mr. Greene. Shelton worked very hard to help you."

"What do you know about it?" he sneered.

More than you want me to know. "Mr. and Mrs. Greene, why don't we make some tea while we wait for Shelton?"

"Hiram, please." Elizabeth placed a loving hand on his arm.

"Oh, all right."

Katherine went to the kitchen, followed by the Greens. "Have you packed away your kitchen belongings yet?"

"No," Elizabeth said. "Since we don't know where we're

going to stay, I thought we'd leave them here for now. I hope Shelton won't mind."

"I don't think he will."

"What gives you the right to tell us what our son is thinking?" Hiram spat.

Katherine squeezed her eyes shut and prayed for God's grace to help her say something that would reflect God's mercy and grace. "Mr. Greene, I took your abusive tongue when I was your servant. But I am not a servant any longer, and I will not be spoken to in that tone."

"And who made you—"

"God did." Katherine placed her hands on her hips. "Now, sit down before my temper really starts to rise."

He sat.

Katherine filled a kettle with water. "You do know that Shelton and I are planning on getting married one day."

Hiram mumbled.

Elizabeth smiled. "Yes, dear, Shelton made that clear when he came back to Hazel Greene."

Katherine put the kettle on the stove. "He and I have spoken openly with each other. He loves you both and respects you tremendously. He's hurting terribly having to make this decision, but he can't support your gambling habit, Mr. Greene."

"Who's asking him to?"

"You are," Katherine stated.

Hiram Greene blanched.

Katherine wasn't sure where she'd found such boldness. Perhaps living with Grandma Mac was rubbing off on her.

"We haven't asked Shelton for any money," Elizabeth interjected.

"True. But your husband has been charging to your son's accounts in town."

Elizabeth stared at him with wide eyes. "Hiram?"

He buried his face in his hands. "I was going to pay it back."

"With what?" Katherine asked.

He sat up straight and squared his shoulders. "With the money I'd earn."

"How? From gambling? How much have you won so far?" Katherine stared at his blank face for a moment before continuing. "That's the problem. You can't think straight when you're gambling. It controls you. I've lived with enough gamblers to know how it works."

"Hiram, is this true?"

He turned his face away from his wife.

Katherine felt sorry for them. "Mrs. Greene, I'm sure your husband didn't set out to become a gambler. It may have started as a gentleman's wager over a horse race or some such thing. He probably made some money in the beginning. Then it began to control him, forcing him to make unwise choices. Fortunately, or unfortunately, you had enough money that he could hide his gambling from the family for years. Shelton says he only learned about it six months before he came here. But I know he's been gambling for at least seven years."

"How do you know that?" Elizabeth asked.

"That's how I came to work for your family. Mr. Greene won me in a poker game."

Tears pooled in Elizabeth's eyes. "Hiram, is this true?"

Hiram pulled at his collar.

Katherine poured the hot water into the teapot and let the tea steep. "Mr. Greene do you really want to throw away your wife, your children, and your grandchildren for a deck of cards?"

He shook his head.

"You have the perfect opportunity to make things right. You can start over. Work with Shelton and help him breed horses. A man with your business sense must know legitimate ways to make a profit."

Hiram Greene cleared his throat. "He wouldn't want me."

Katherine chuckled. "He knows all about my past, and he wants me. You both raised a wonderful son who has become a man with such respect for his parents that he wouldn't listen to me when I said you should pay for your own mistakes. Instead, he convinced me that the right thing to do was to love and honor you by helping you and by having you move into this house."

Katherine poured tea into each cup, then added milk the way she knew the Greens liked it. She was serving them now as a free woman, out of love for God and gratitude for what He'd done for her, not out of a debt that Hiram Greene once held over her. Katherine knew beyond a doubt she was totally free from the bondage of the past. *Thank You, Lord.*

"Mr. and Mrs. Greene, there's something else you should know." She sat across from the couple. "I love Shelton, and I know now that I can truly love him without fear from the past." She looked Hiram straight in the eye. She could tell from the look on his face that he realized she was recalling the night when he threatened her. "I thank you for all you've done to raise my future husband. I will be honored to have him as my partner in life. Even your mistakes have made him strong."

Katherine pushed the chair away from the table and stood. "Mr. Greene, this is your house, if you choose to let the Lord rebuild you." Katherine laid a hand on Elizabeth's shoulder and gave a gentle squeeze. "I'll see myself out."

❧

Shelton found he owed more than a hundred dollars in town, thanks to his father's charging. He had money left from the sale of the property in Hazel Greene, so he made arrangements to pay off each debt. But he made it clear that he would not accept any further charges on his father's behalf.

He didn't know whether he'd find his parents at the house or not, but he hoped he would. He'd spoken harshly with his father earlier, and he wanted to make peace with the man before he left.

He'd hoped Katherine would agree to marry him since Parson Kincaid had suggested it. But she was right; a new marriage was hard enough. They shouldn't start with his parents and their problems weighing them down. He couldn't be his father's guardian any longer. Until the man's heart changed and he repented of his sin, nothing would be different.

When he arrived back at the house, he sighed with relief that his parents were home. But the conversation he had with them took an unexpected turn.

"Shelton, I need to apologize to you," Hiram said. "I've made a mess of my life and squandered my family's fortune. Katherine opened my eyes, with a little help from your mother." He glanced at his wife, then turned back to Shelton. "She doesn't let a man off the hook, does she?"

Shelton chuckled. "No, she doesn't."

"You'll have your hands full with that one, son. But she's right. I do want to change."

"Katherine told me your father's been gambling for at least seven years," Elizabeth said. "He confessed that it's been nine. Does that sound right with what you saw in the financial books?"

"Yes," he reluctantly admitted.

"Your father has agreed not to touch the finances. I'm going to pay all the bills and he'll help me decide how and which ones."

"Dad, are you aware of the debt you've incurred in Creelsboro?"

Hiram hung his head in shame, then lifted it again and faced Shelton. "Yes. About a hundred dollars, give or take a few."

Elizabeth gasped. "Do we have that kind of money?"

"I do," Shelton acknowledged. "I've made arrangements with the businessmen in town. I should have it all paid off in time for Christmas."

Hiram's shoulders slumped. Then he lifted them and looked directly into his son's eyes. "Shelton, I know it won't be easy, but I'm willing to work at changing."

"It'll only happen by God's grace, Dad. You can't do this in your own strength. Trust me, I've tried."

Hiram nodded.

Elizabeth took her husband's hand. "Shelton, your father and I have a lot to talk about. Will you excuse us?"

"Of course. Good night." He stood. "I'm glad you're going to stay."

❧

Shelton was restless all night. Unable to sleep, he took an early-morning stroll through the woods and down to the river. Ice-covered rocks lined the river's edge.

He turned up the collar on his coat and walked north around the peninsula that stuck out into the Cumberland. It felt good to own property. In spite of all his father had done to waste the family's wealth, Shelton had the potential to earn it back again. The problem would be keeping that from becoming his primary purpose in life.

As he rounded the peninsula, he found an inlet with calm water and an embankment that climbed up twenty-five to thirty feet. Shelton climbed up the steep terrain. From the top, he could see his house to the left. The breathtaking view was spectacular. "This is where I'll build, Lord. Katherine deserves a beautiful house with a wonderful view. She'll love it here."

With single-minded determination he set about making his plans. He would build a cabin with a loft. Upstairs would be their bedroom. From there they could see water all around them.

Shelton walked to Urias's house. By the time he arrived the sun was up over the eastern ridge. "Urias?" he called as he entered the barn.

"Over here."

Shelton stepped into the darkened barn. The smell of freshly spread hay made him realize he needed to do the same in his own barn. Urias sat by the cow, milking her.

"Have your parents moved out?"

Shelton filled Urias in about the latest turn of events. "If Father follows through on his promises, it looks like he and Mother will be living in the house permanently. Of course, if Katherine and I get married, it'll be tough living under the same roof with them. But we'll have to. . .at least until I can build a house for the two of us."

Urias leaned back and raked his hair with his fingers. "Before you and Katherine started developing a relationship, Mac and I were building a log cabin for her a little to the west of Grandma Mac's house. She wanted so much to have her own home."

Shelton knew about that desire.

"We got as far as putting up the sides, but haven't put a roof on yet. What do you think about you two living there for a couple of years while you build your own home?"

"My parents could use the privacy."

"And so could you and Katherine." Urias described the cabin's location and the work they had accomplished so far. The weather was too cold to put on the roof right away, but come spring, it could be finished within a day or two. Shelton wondered if Katherine would be ready to marry by spring.

As he made his way to Grandma Mac's house, he wondered if he should take Urias up on the offer of the log cabin or if he should just build his own house on the peninsula overlooking the river. He couldn't wait to consult Katherine.

"Good morning, Mrs. MacKenneth," he said when she opened the door to him.

"Morning, Shelton," she said, escorting him into the living room. "You're up early."

I haven't gone to sleep, he held back from telling her. "Is Katherine up?"

"Haven't seen her yet this morning. What happened last night?"

"I'm not sure. That's why I need to talk with her."

"I'll go fetch her. You set for a spell. You look exhausted."

Shelton paced in the sitting area until Katherine entered, wearing her housecoat. "Is everything all right?"

"It's fine. I didn't mean to worry you."

"What's the matter? Why are you here so early?"

"I have to ask you a couple of questions about your conversation with my parents last night."

Katherine tensed.

"Honey, relax. Whatever you said did wonders. Father is repentant. Mother is in shock. They both want to stay. Is that all right with you? I mean, it's your house, too, or at least it will be."

"Shelton, sit down." Katherine coaxed him to the chair and she sat in the rocking chair. "It's not my house, Shelton." Tears formed in her eyes. "It never will be."

"Why? What's happened?"

❧

"I can't really explain this," Katherine said, "but yesterday, when I was speaking with your parents, I realized the house would never truly be mine. It's theirs. You probably think I'm missing some mental capacities, and I probably am, but—"

Shelton placed a finger to her lips and smiled. "I know what you mean. I was out this morning exploring my—I mean our—property, and I found what I think will be the ideal place for us to build our home one day. Unfortunately, it will be a couple years before I have the funds to build the kind of house I'd like for us."

Katherine blinked. "Two years?"

"Yes."

"We have to wait two years?" she repeated. Didn't he know she'd be happy living just about anywhere with him? *Except in his parents' house*, she amended.

Shelton flushed. "Well, we could get married in the spring if you don't mind living in something temporarily."

"What are you saying?"

"Apparently, Mac and Urias started building a log cabin for you a while back. Urias told me about it this morning. The roof isn't on, but we could put one on in the spring. It's small, but it would be big enough for us to use for a while. What do you think?"

"I think this family tries to help each other a little too much."

Shelton chuckled. "You're probably right. But you didn't answer my question."

"I'm not sure. It sounds promising, but. . ."

Not wanting her to talk herself out of getting married next spring, he changed the subject. "So, what did you say to my parents?"

Katherine gave a detailed account of the things she'd said to the Greens. "We still have some issues to deal with regarding your parents. We can't be paying up every time your father slips up and gambles."

"We have to trust them."

"I can't, Shelton. Not yet. I need more time."

sixteen

For two weeks Katherine found various ways to avoid Shelton's parents. The Christmas season provided an excellent excuse. She had gifts to make and embroidery and needlepoint to finish.

She knew Shelton no longer believed her excuses. He hadn't pushed her, but he stopped inviting her to come to the house and have dinner with him and his parents.

But on Christmas Eve, meeting with the family was unavoidable. The O'Learys, the Greens, and the MacKenneths were all getting together at Urias's house tonight. Katherine packed the last of her gifts in the satchel.

"Katherine?" Grandma Mac called from the bottom of the stairs.

"Yes?" Katherine tied the bag closed and placed the strap over her shoulder.

"Shelton is here."

Katherine stood at the top of the stairs and looked down at the elderly woman. If she and Shelton got married in the spring, Katherine realized, Grandma Mac would have to move in with Mac and Pam. "I'm ready."

Shelton stepped up behind Grandma Mac and placed his hands on her shoulders. "She's mighty pretty, ain't she?" Shelton winked.

"Isn't she," Grandma Mac corrected with a light tap on his knuckles.

Katherine held back a giggle.

"She's very pretty, isn't she?" he amended.

Grandma Mac smacked him on his backside with her cane. "Go load those packages by the door into the wagon."

"Yes, ma'am."

After he left, Grandma Mac whispered to Katherine, "Two can play at that game. Notice, he didn't get a chance to kiss you yet."

"What did I do to deserve such treatment?" Katherine said, enjoying their little repartee.

"You encouraged him. I saw the twinkle in your eyes. I may be getting on in years, but you can't fool me."

Katherine giggled. "No, ma'am."

Outside, they climbed into the carriage. Shelton provided several wool blankets and a large bearskin to wrap around Grandma Mac.

"Mac sent this, didn't he?"

"Yes, ma'am. He didn't want you getting too cold on the way to Urias's."

"Humph. I dressed in layers."

Shelton draped the bearskin around her anyway.

"Can I join you under there?" Katherine asked, shivering.

The old woman clucked her tongue as she lifted the blanket for Katherine. "You young folks don't know how to weather the elements. Why, back in my day. . ." Grandma Mac instructed them on cold weather survival all the way to Urias's.

Shelton brought the carriage to a stop at their destination and escorted Grandma Mac to the front door.

A hint of jealousy swept over Katherine at the sight of someone else in Shelton's arms. How long had it been since she'd been in his embrace? She sighed and managed to wiggle her way out of the bearskin covering and retrieve her satchel from under the bench.

Shelton came up behind her and wrapped her in his arms. "I missed you." He kissed the nape of her neck.

Katherine turned in his arms and faced him. "I've missed you, too. I'm actually jealous of Grandma Mac."

"Really?" Shelton chortled. "She's a great old woman, but not my type."

"Grandpa Mac must have had his hands full with her."

Shelton released her, and an instant chill washed over her. "No doubt about it." He reached behind the bench and gathered Grandma Mac's packages. "What did she make?"

"I don't know. She's been rather secretive."

He eyed her satchel. "What about you?"

"You'll have to wait and see," she teased. "But your present isn't in here."

"It's not?" He grabbed a third package.

"I saved it for later, for just the two of us."

A smile spread across his lips and lit up his blue eyes.

Lord, I love that smile.

"Then you'll have to wait to receive your gift, too."

"When can we slip away?"

"Honey, if I had my way, we would have slipped away ages ago." He leaned over and gave her a quick kiss. "We need to talk, but it's freezing out here. And if I don't bring Grandma Mac's packages inside she'll skin me alive."

Katherine relaxed again and chuckled. "Aye, that be your lot for sure."

They scurried into the warm house. The family members sat in the living room while the children ran up and down the hallway. The air seemed alive with excitement. . .until she caught a glimpse of Hiram Greene's eyes.

Katherine's back tightened and she felt the color drain from her face. How could she live like this for the rest of her life?

❧

Shelton leaned against the living room wall. He noticed

Katherine's demeanor change as soon as she walked into the house. *Why?*

Everyone else seemed full of cheer. Even his parents were enjoying their grandchildren. He gently rubbed the back of her neck. "Are you all right?" he whispered in her ear.

She turned and looked at him. Her lively green eyes reflected a deep sadness. He pulled her into his embrace. "Whatever it is, it will be all right."

Katherine shook her head.

Lord, help me. I don't understand what has Katherine so upset. His mind flickered back over the moments before they entered the house. Everything was fine. She had been happy, excited, playful. What could have changed?

The rumble of laughter and merriment dissolved into an expectant hush as Mac cleared his throat and stood. "Grandma Mac, as the matriarch of the family, would you please read Luke's account of Jesus's birth?"

Grandma Mac's weathered face lit up. "I'd be happy to."

Shelton slipped out of the family room with Katherine in tow. "Come on. We should talk."

Katherine planted her feet. "Not now," she whispered. "Later."

He didn't want to wait. He wanted to deal with whatever was bothering her immediately. But he also didn't want to make a scene and have the entire family in on their discussion. He let her go back to the living room. But instead of joining her, he left by the back door and headed to the barn.

For the past month, since his father had decided to quit gambling, Shelton's time with Katherine had become almost nonexistent. His parents, the house, the barn, and the horses all needed him. He'd been working with his mother on their finances, trying to teach her how to keep records and ledger sheets. Father had never let her be a part of the financial picture, and there were many little details she had to understand. In addition, Shelton was busy every day working on the land, preparing it for next year's planting. If only he had more time.

Kehoe stood in his stall, noisily munching on oats.

"Hey, boy, how you doing?"

Kehoe's silence emanated unquestioned loyalty and acceptance.

"I can't stay in here." Shelton patted the animal's neck. "Katherine and I need more time together."

Kehoe shook his head and snorted.

"You're right. I should be inside with her. I don't like it much when she shuts me out."

Kehoe took half a step sideways, leaving little room for Shelton.

He chuckled. "All right, boy, I get the message."

He turned toward the barn door and found Urias standing there, his hands draped across his chest. "Pru sent me out to get you to come back inside and join the festivities. What's the problem?"

"Nothing."

"If I believed that, I'd be dumber than a stump. Are you and Katherine having trouble?"

Shelton clapped Urias on the back. "Nothing that can't be solved with time and a little conversation."

Urias's green eyes fixed on Shelton. He squared up his shoulders, his posture like a soldier standing at attention. "Fine, I'll trust you. But don't hurt her. She's had enough trouble in her life."

They made their way back to the house. As he entered the living room, Shelton smiled at Katherine. She turned away. His heart sank. *Dear Lord, don't let me lose her.*

❧

Katherine buried herself under the covers. A chill nipped her nose. The house creaked against frequent gusts of wind.

Christmas morning had arrived. But she didn't feel much like celebrating. All night she'd battled conflicting emotions. Her love for Shelton. His love for her. Hiram Greene's disdain. Would she ever be free from the past? The bondage she'd been in for so many years was gone. But the anger in Hiram Green's eyes led her to believe she'd never be able to marry Shelton. How could she bring children into this world when their only grandfather hated her so?

"Why do I have to keep going over the same things, Lord? When will I be truly satisfied and accept myself as someone You cherish? As someone Shelton cherishes? Why does it have to be so hard? Will I ever stop overreacting when people like Hiram Greene glare at me?"

Katherine threw off the covers and jumped out of bed. Her fur-lined slippers, a gift from Mac and Pam a couple of Christmases ago, gloved her feet. They were getting thin on the bottom and she could use a new pair, but she'd never felt the freedom to ask for anything for herself.

"Katherine?" Grandma Mac called out. Her voice sounded weak and shaky.

She bolted out of her room. "Where are you?"

"In my room, dear. I'm all right. I'm just a bit unsteady on my feet."

Katherine ran to Grandma Mac's room and saw the older woman holding on to the tall bedpost. "What's the matter?"

"I'm just old, and stayed up too late, I suspect. Would you help me get ready for Christmas dinner? I want to wear my red dress and white lace shawl, the one Pam and Mac gave me last year."

Katherine offered a steadying hand. "Why don't you sit in the chair and I'll get your things."

"Thank you," Grandma Mac sighed as she sat.

Katherine's heart pounded in her chest. She'd feared something like this would happen one day. Age had a way of creeping up on folks, but Grandma Mac never seemed as old as she really was.

She moved to the closet and glanced back at the old woman. Grandma Mac's chest moved up and down in slow, labored breaths. "Are you certain you're all right?"

The woman's brown eyes seemed darker. "Perhaps I should rest."

"We've got plenty of time, Grandma Mac," she said, returning to the woman's side. "Here, let me help you back into bed."

Blue-veined hands patted Katherine's arm. "Thank you."

Katherine helped Grandma Mac settle into bed. *Father God, please be with Grandma Mac and heal her,* she prayed over and over. She hoped someone would come to call on them. Last night, the group had decided that each family would spend the early-morning hours at home, then gather at Urias's house for a late breakfast while they waited for the Christmas dinner to cook. Not that she wanted to spend any more time with Hiram Greene and his accusing scowls.

Katherine paced and nibbled her fingernails. "Lord, please make Grandma Mac well."

Tea! The idea hit her hard. She ran to the cabinets and looked through the various tins and glass jars. Mac always claimed tea helped a person get going in the morning. Personally, she didn't care for the stuff. It tasted too much like the roots and dirt it had grown from. But she had to confess, it did give her a boost when she didn't feel quite herself.

She pushed things around until she found the little blue tin. She positioned the kettle on the stove and added some wood to the cooling embers, found a tea rag, and measured out a rounded teaspoon. She placed the spoonful of leaves in the center of the tea-stained cloth and tied a thin cotton string around it. Then she set it in the china teapot that Grandma Mac claimed came from England as a gift from her grandmother, who had received it from her mother as a wedding present.

Katherine put a tray together and rummaged through the room for things to decorate the tray for the festive holiday. She placed the tip of a pine branch in the corner with a hand-painted red glass ball that Grandma Mac said had been a gift from Grandpa Mac on their fifth Christmas together.

With the tray set, she carried it to Grandma Mac's bedroom. When she pressed the door open, she saw Grandma Mac sleeping comfortably. Her breathing was even, less labored.

A loud rattle at the front door echoed through the house. Katherine set the tray on a table and went to the front door. When she opened it, Hiram Greene's eyes locked with hers. Katherine shrank back against the wall.

seventeen

"Merry Christmas, Katherine," Shelton said as he worked his way around his father. Her stance reminded him of a frightened filly plastered against the back wall of a corral. "Honey, what's the matter?"

She looked at the floor. "Grandma Mac isn't feeling well." She slowly lifted her head. "If you stay with her, I'll get Pam and Mac."

He laid a reassuring hand on her forearm. "I'll go. You stay here and take care of her."

She glanced at his father. Her shoulders squared off as if bracing herself against some unseen horror. Shelton's mind flicked back across the stories Katherine had revealed about her past. Had his father abused her? No. Katherine had been clear on that. Then what had he done or said that made her so leery of him?

"I'll go." Hiram stepped out of the doorway and back onto the front porch.

Katherine visibly relaxed.

As his father climbed into the wagon, Shelton inched closer to Katherine. "Hi." He lightly brushed his lips against her satin cheek. "Merry Christmas."

"It hasn't been merry so far," she mumbled.

"Katherine, we have to talk."

"Not now," she protested, and slipped past him into the living room.

"When?" He reached for her. She flinched from his touch. He debated removing his hand, then waited a moment longer, hoping she would relax under his grip. Thankfully, she did.

"Shelton, I can't marry you."

"Pardon?"

"Your father will never accept our relationship. I won't put myself in a position of wondering every day of my life if you will begin resenting me because of your father's disdain for me and who I was."

"I don't care what my father thinks."

"Yes, you do." She cupped his cheek. "Your entire existence revolves around making certain everything is all right with them. They are your top priority."

He opened his mouth to protest. Her fingers on his lips stopped him.

"You should see the anger in your father's eyes whenever he looks at me. It's just like that time. . ." She cut off her words and walked away from him.

Shelton came up behind her and held her in a loving embrace. "What did he do to you?"

"Nothing."

Shelton spun her around to face him. "I don't believe that."

Tears welled in her eyes. She looked at her feet. He bent his knees and lifted her chin. "Katherine, look at me."

The tears fell and streamed down her face. "In your father's eyes, I will always be a servant. Think about how your family has treated servants in the past. We were possessions, cattle. We were not people with our own thoughts and desires. You're a part of that. You've treated your servants like that too—even me."

"You were never. . ." He let his words trail off. She was right. He had treated her like a servant. He had ordered her about the way he did all the others. Until he fell in love with her. "I can't accept that it's not possible for us to marry, Katherine. I admit there will be hardship at times, but God is the Lord of our lives. He'll help us."

"Perhaps. But Hiram Greene will always stand in the way," she said with a boldness he'd never heard from her.

Shelton's heart pounded. How could this be, after all this time of being patient, gently coaxing her like a skittish mare? "I love you, Katherine. Nothing should stand in opposition to that. Except God. And I believe He brought us together."

"I'm sorry, Shelton. I just can't."

He wanted to argue, but what would that accomplish? Instead, he gave her a passionate kiss. "If you ever change your mind, you know how to find me." With all the strength he could muster, he left.

God, he prayed as he climbed up on Kehoe, *move in Katherine's heart. There's nothing more I can do.*

❧

Three long days had passed since she'd pushed Shelton out of her life. Katherine craved his touch and affection.

She'd burned a lot of wood since Christmas, trying to keep the house warm for Grandma Mac. The wood boxes by the fireplace were nearly empty. She grabbed her winter coat and braced for the damp chill that had blown in from the north last night.

Arriving at the woodshed, she noticed there were only two cords under the protection of the shelter. She loaded the canvas carrier and brought it into the house. She repeated the process three more times until the wood boxes in the house were full.

Rubbing her hands together for warmth, she ventured back outside and moved a cord of wood from the elements to the protection of the woodshed. "Oh, how I miss Shelton," she moaned. *Father, I don't understand. Why did I let myself fall in love with a man I could never be with?*

"Good morning, Katherine." Urias stepped up beside her.

"Let me take care of that."

She gratefully stood back to let him handle the heavy bundle.

"So tell me," he said, putting on his leather work gloves, "what's happened between you and Shelton?"

"There's nothing to tell. We've simply agreed we aren't right for each other."

Urias peered at her. "Interesting. He said you broke off the engagement."

Katherine felt the sting of her reddened face. She knew it had nothing to do with the northern winds, but from her own shame of being slightly deceptive with her brother. "Yes, I suppose I did."

"Do you mind if I ask why?"

Katherine took a step back. "Urias, how do you deal with Hiram Greene?"

"Like I told you before, I honor the man simply because he is Prudence's father."

"I tried that, but it didn't work."

"It isn't just about honor. You need to forgive Hiram."

"I did," she said.

"Then what's the problem?"

"Did you see the way he looked at me on Christmas Eve when I walked into your house?"

Urias hauled an armful of logs to the shed. "No. How did he look?"

"Like I was the cause of all his problems."

Urias dropped the wood onto the floor. "Fact is, you are a major part of his current situation. Thanks to you, his wife now knows the full details of his gambling habit."

"That's not my fault," she defended.

He placed a loving hand on her shoulder. "Katherine, we are called to forgive those who have sinned against us. You should pray and ask God if you really have forgiven him."

"I can't make Shelton decide between me and his parents."

Urias massaged her shoulder for a moment. "Katherine, you do needlepoint. What's on the surface is pretty. The tangled mess of threads underneath is not. Being a bondservant was a horrific experience. I understand that. But God is weaving you into a new tapestry. The redemptive power of His blood is like the piece of fabric you sew on. The finished needlepoint is what you're becoming. But that doesn't negate the tangled mess that's under that cloth."

Katherine sighed.

"Forgiveness is a process. Hiram Greene must go through his own process as well. But you can't live your life based on the changes going on in another person."

Urias's words grated. She knew her fears were to blame for her decision, but she couldn't see any other choice.

"You have to decide whether or not you think Shelton is a gift the Lord is giving you. If he is, grab on to him and don't let him go."

She wanted that with all her heart. But it couldn't be that simple, could it? "I'll think about it."

"Good. Now, why don't you go on inside and make some coffee while I finish up here. I'm going to need something hot today. Mac says we could be in for a cold snap."

Back inside the house she prepared Urias's coffee, then went to check on Grandma Mac. The woman's illness had been a blessing, in a way. In her weakened condition, Grandma Mac hadn't been able to chastise her about calling a halt to her engagement with Shelton.

Grandma Mac sat in her rocking chair next to the window, reading her Bible.

"How are you feeling?" Katherine asked.

"Better. I don't know what came over me. I was fit as a

fiddle one moment and worn out like an old shoe the next."

Katherine smiled. "Can I make you some breakfast?"

"A poached egg on toast would be nice."

"Would you like to eat in your room?"

"No, dear. I think I'd better start moving or these old bones will set in place."

"I doubt that." Katherine chuckled, then bid a hasty retreat to the kitchen. She busied herself with the breakfast preparation, trying to ignore Urias's words, which echoed over and over in her head.

What angered her more than Urias's advice was that Shelton hadn't stopped by for the past three days. She missed their times together. She missed being in his arms.

Urias and Grandma Mac took up most of the conversation around the breakfast table, giving Katherine some relief.

"Thank you for the coffee and the eggs," Urias said as he pushed his chair back and stood. "But I must be off. I'm working on the cabin this morning."

"Why?" Katherine asked.

Urias placed his coonskin cap on his head. "Because you want a place of your own, remember?"

"Yes, but. . ." She and Shelton were supposed to have moved in there after they married. But that wasn't going to happen.

Urias gave her shoulder a loving squeeze. "Even if you and Shelton don't marry, I want you to have your own home."

Katherine swallowed her emotions and simply nodded.

Urias patted her shoulder and left. Grandma Mac rose from the table and took her plate to the sink.

"Let me do that," Katherine protested.

"I'm fine. But it appears you're not. Want to tell me about it?"

"There's not much to tell. Shelton and I agreed it wasn't wise for us to get married."

Grandma Mac peered at Katherine in a way that said, *"Fess up."*

"All right. I told Shelton we couldn't get married. I can't live with Hiram Greene's attitude toward me."

"You know, I did notice Hiram's appearance change when you entered the house on Christmas Eve. But I don't believe he was reacting in quite the way you think. That man is a troubled soul. But from what I hear, he's working hard to get right with his family and, I dare say, his Maker. You, on the other hand, seem to be living in fear again. Am I right?"

❧

"How is she?" Shelton asked as Urias joined him at the log cabin.

"Miserable. Same as you. Why don't you go talk to her?"

Shelton pounded the nail harder, sinking it with one swing. Taking another from his nail apron, he tapped then sank it deep in the wood. The cold temperatures made working this time of year hard on a person, but he needed to burn off his anger so he could wait patiently. "Katherine has to come to me. I think it's important for her to step out in order to get past all she's been through and know she has the right to approach me."

"This isn't about you. It's about your father."

"I'm aware of that." Feeling the tension rise, Shelton moved over to the saw and cut the next plank. "And he knows what he's done. He wanted to apologize to her on Christmas morning, but Katherine overreacted. Honestly, I thought she was afraid he'd beat her. Urias, if she can't conquer these fears, our marriage really would be a mistake."

"You're probably right. But you're as stubborn as she is, you know."

Shelton chuckled.

Urias picked up a plank for the window frame. "If you two aren't going to get married, why is it so important for us to get this cabin ready right now? Katherine seems to enjoy living with Grandma Mac."

The cut end of the board fell to the floor. Shelton wiped the sweat from his brow. "While I was praying about our broken engagement, I felt like the Lord was impressing on me to give Katherine what she's wanted for so long. I don't believe she wants to be alone. She only thinks she does. But she won't know that if she's never given the chance."

"I reckon you know what you're doing. But why couldn't we wait until spring?"

"I'm hoping she'll come to her senses by then and marry me."

Urias grinned.

They worked long and hard until noon. "I have to go," Urias said. "I'll be back tomorrow."

Shelton extended his hand. "Thanks for the help."

"You're welcome. It should be ready by next week."

"I hope so. I still want to bring in some wood or coal for heat."

"We can help with that." Urias pulled a small pouch from his pocket. "Pru and I set aside a small amount to help you with the expenses."

Shelton didn't want to take the money but knew it would come in handy. "Thank you."

After a quick meal Shelton went back to work on the log cabin. He had filled all the joints with clay, the roof was on, and the only remaining things to be done were small.

Mac joined him for three hours in the afternoon. By dinnertime Shelton put away his tools and headed for home.

As he arrived at the old farmhouse, he couldn't help but think of Katherine. She'd gone out of her way to work on the place and get it ready for him and his parents. *Lord, she has a wonderful heart. Please help her get past this overwhelming fear.*

In the barn, he checked on Kate and the twins. His gut

tightened another notch as he remembered the night Katherine helped with the delivery. He brushed the dust off his clothes before entering the house.

His mother stood by the kitchen stove. "Did you have a good day, son?"

"We got a lot accomplished."

"Good. Your father's in the den. He'd like to speak with you. We'll be eating in thirty minutes. Be sure and clean up before you come to the table."

"Yes, ma'am."

Shelton collected his thoughts as he walked to the den. His father sat in a high-backed stuffed chair that Katherine had refinished. "Mother said you wished to speak with me."

"Yes. I must confess I've been rather displeased with your desire to marry Kate."

"Katherine," Shelton corrected.

Hiram Greene nodded and motioned for Shelton to take a seat. "And when you pushed me to apologize on Christmas, I admit I was doing it to please you, not because I agreed with it. But your mother and I have been doing a lot of talking lately. She's a wise woman."

Shelton could imagine his mother giving his father a piece of her mind. He'd been on the receiving end of her lectures many times. It seemed strange that she'd never spoken to her husband in the same way.

"I'm a proud man, Shelton, so this isn't easy for me. But. . ." Hiram stopped.

"Father?"

"What I mean to say is, what can I do to make things right between you and Katherine?"

If only Katherine could hear this. "I still think you should apologize to her. But as for our relationship—it's in the Lord's hands." *And Katherine's.*

"Very well. But if there's anything else I can do, let me know."

"Thanks, Dad. Mother said dinner would be ready in thirty minutes. Guess I'd better wash up." Shelton excused himself and went to his room. He poured water into the basin, then stripped off his soiled clothes and tossed them in a heap.

Washed and refreshed, he dressed in a clean set of white flannels, dark trousers, and a white shirt. With his hair semi-dry, he combed it back. After a quick examination in the mirror he decided he looked more like he was heading for Sunday morning vespers than for dinner with his family. Dressing up for the evening meal had been a regularity back in Hazel Greene, but since moving to Jamestown, the occasions had been few.

He went downstairs and was about to enter the dining room when a knock on the front door distracted him. He pulled the door open. His heart stopped.

eighteen

Katherine didn't know whether she was shaking more from fear or the cold, but seeing Shelton standing there all dressed up made her want to leap into his arms.

"Katherine."

She fought the desire to jump into his embrace. "Hi."

Shelton beamed. "Come on in."

Katherine squeezed her eyes shut and braved the step over the threshold of Shelton's home. Her legs wobbled but somehow managed to move forward. *Why does it have to be this hard?*

"We're about to eat dinner. Would you like to join us?"

"No, no. I can come back." Katherine spun around.

Shelton grabbed her wrist. His light touch crumbled her resolve.

"I just came to say I'm sorry, Shelton. And I miss you. But. . ."

"Honey, I told you I would wait." He inched closer.

Katherine wanted to nuzzle into his embrace. But she hesitated. She'd felt guilty all day. She couldn't change her feelings toward his father, or calm her fears. They came from a place where she had no control. They sprang up in her even when she didn't want them to.

Shelton caressed the back of her neck with his fingers. "I love you."

She collapsed in his arms. Tears ran down onto his shirt. She inhaled deeply, taking in the scent of his cologne. "I wish I could love you back," she mumbled.

"You will. Give it time." Shelton pulled back slightly. "Your log cabin will be ready by the end of the week. You'll have your dream home, Katherine, a place all to yourself, just like you wanted."

Katherine wept so hard she couldn't speak.

"Mother," Shelton called out, "you and Father go ahead and start the evening meal without me."

Katherine sensed his parents watching from the next room. She should probably stand up straight and remove herself from his shoulder. But nothing mattered at this moment except being in the loving embrace of the man she loved.

Shelton drove her back to Grandma Mac's home. They didn't talk. She knew Shelton was a patient man. She'd watched him work with his horses, firm yet never getting cross. A quiet strength seemed to emanate from him.

She drew on that strength to help her gain the courage to leave the wagon and enter Grandma Mac's home. He walked her to the door and kissed her lightly on the cheek. "Good night, Katherine. I'll see you soon."

She entered the darkened house and went straight to her room. She couldn't face Grandma Mac tonight. She couldn't face herself. She'd gone to Shelton's house to make things right between them. But how could she when fear wrapped its stringy threads around her heart?

❧

Three days later Katherine moved into her own house. Every member of the family came to help her settle in. She found traces of everyone's handiwork around the new log cabin. It had been a labor of love.

She had received the desire of her heart. But after her first night in the log cabin, she felt more alone than ever before.

A knock on the front door sent her running. She smiled excitedly, expecting Shelton. She opened the door to Hiram

Greene. Her smile dropped.

"May I come in?"

She held on to the doorknob. "What can I help you with, Mr. Greene?"

"I came to apologize."

"Pardon?"

"Please let me come inside, Katherine. There are some things you should know."

Katherine took in a deep breath and stepped aside. "Can I get you some coffee? Tea?"

"No, thank you. I'll get right to the point."

Hiram admitted his guilt with regard to her position in society and asked her forgiveness for every inappropriate thing he'd ever said to her. "Please forgive me. I see now that you and Shelton have a special love. I hope it's not too late."

Katherine's voice caught in her throat. "I forgive you." What else could she do? God required it. She told Urias she had done it. So why did it seem so stiff and forced?

Hiram smiled and gave a curt nod of his head. "I'll be on my way then. Thank you for your time, Miss O'Leary."

Katherine followed her unexpected guest to the front door and watched as he climbed into the saddle and rode away. Her world seemed to spin. One moment she thought she was doing what was best. Then it all fell back in her lap. She had to decide if she could truly forgive Hiram Greene and trust Shelton and his love enough for them to build a marriage.

But she hadn't seen Shelton much since Christmas morning. Had she gone too far? Would he still take her back? *Lord, I've made such a mess of my life. Please help me.*

❧

The next month was the hardest one Shelton had ever lived through. Every fiber of his being wanted to be with Katherine, but he still felt the Lord was asking him to wait. And he had, even after he knew that his father had spoken with her and apologized. Still, she didn't come. For days he tried to conjure up ways they could "accidentally" meet, but he knew he shouldn't.

Urias and the others checked on Katherine in her new home from time to time, and she visited with Grandma Mac nearly every day. Yet she still kept her distance from him. *Why?* It didn't make sense, at least not to his way of thinking.

He spent a lot of time with his horses. The twin foals were growing every day. Mr. Crockett purchased the colt, although Shelton would continue to raise them for a time.

Shelton saddled Kehoe and rode to the spit of land overlooking the Cumberland River. "Forgive me, Lord, but I can't wait any longer. I have to know what she's thinking, what she's feeling." He turned Kehoe in the direction of Katherine's log cabin. He saw her a little ways ahead, sitting on a large boulder overlooking the river.

"Katherine!" he hollered.

She smiled and waved.

Shelton jumped off Kehoe and hustled up to the side of the rock. "What are you doing here?"

"I come here to pray sometimes." She looked at her folded hands in her lap. "Your father came to see me."

"He spoke with me after he visited you." He sat on the rock beside her.

"I've missed you," she confessed.

Renewed hope surged through his heart. "I've missed you, too. How's your new cottage?"

"Horrible."

"Horrible? What's the matter? You should have told me sooner. I would have come and fixed whatever the problem is."

She let out half a chuckle. "No, you can't fix this, Shelton. It's me. I've found that I don't like living alone."

Shelton raised his eyebrows. "Ah, Katherine, I can fix that. Just give the word and we'll marry."

She took his hand. "I know. That's why I didn't come to you. God gave me the desire of my heart to have my own home. I felt I should live there for a while and make peace with my mistakes."

"Mistakes?"

She raised her fingers to his lips. "I wanted my own place for selfish reasons. I wasn't appreciating everything the Lord had already given me. I was taking it all for granted, complaining, murmuring like the Jews on their way to the Promised Land from enslavement in Egypt. I've been trying to learn to be content with what I have and what's been given to me. I can't be a good wife to you if I'm not content with myself."

"I respect that. But wouldn't it be better if we spent time with each other, and with my family, in order for you to be comfortable with them and with me?"

"That's exactly what I've been trying to get up the courage to ask you."

Shelton pulled her to himself. "I love you, Katherine," he whispered as his lips captured hers.

As the passion rose, she placed her hands on his chest and pushed back some. "I love you, too."

"Then tell me you'll marry me." *Please don't push me away again.*

Slowly she raised her head and leveled those incredible green eyes with his. "I will."

He pulled her closer and held her so tight he feared he'd break her ribs. He relaxed his grip. "When?"

"As soon as possible."

"Today?"

"If you wish."

"Really?" He jumped up. "Come, let's tell the family." He

reached down to help her up.

She continued to sit. "I have something to ask you first."

Please, Lord. Don't let her doubt and fears take over. He sat back down. The rock seemed colder this time.

❧

Lord, I hope I'm not being too forward here, she prayed. "Shel—can I call you that?"

He let out a nervous chuckle. "You can call me anything you'd like."

"If you don't mind, I'd like to get married privately. I'm not opposed to your family being a part of our special day, but I've thought about this for a while now. It seems you and I have always been involved with the family. Every holiday, every big event, we're surrounded by them. Not that it's bad, and after a month of living on my own, I really do appreciate the people who care about me. But. . ."

"I think I understand, and no, I don't mind. We could leave tomorrow for Creelsboro, get the parson to marry us, then take a steamer along the Cumberland River. What do you think?"

"Can you afford it?"

"I sold the colt to Mr. Crockett. That should more than cover the cost."

The idea of being alone with Shelton for several days thrilled her. "I like it. You don't mind?"

"No. But if my sister learns of our plans, the whole family will come running down to the church."

"True." Was it right to be so selfish? "Perhaps we should invite them."

"No. But we should probably tell someone of our plans. I'll swear Father to secrecy. If anyone can keep a secret, he can."

It seemed odd to trust Hiram Greene with any part of her future, but she knew she had to get over those lingering doubts. She nodded her agreement. "Do whatever you think is best."

"Tomorrow it is, then."

"Yes."

"Pack a trunk. I'll ride into Creelsboro and make arrangements with the parson and check on the steamer schedules."

With a boldness she'd only seen in herself once before, she pulled Shelton into a kiss. His arms wrapped around her. *Thank You, Lord, for this tremendous gift.*

❧

The next morning Katherine dressed in the ivory satin wedding dress. The problem was, how to keep Shelton from seeing it until she met him at the altar? There were definite disadvantages to not having a family wedding, she mused. But she was still convinced that their union should be just between the two of them. And while she knew from Hiram's own mouth that he would not oppose the wedding, she still wondered if he would be having second thoughts during the wedding service.

When she heard Shelton's wagon drive up to the house, she covered the dress as best she could with her woolen coat and put her ribbon-and-pearl headpiece, ivory silk gloves, and laced veil into a large cloth purse. Then she reached into the hand-carved box she used to keep under the floorboards of Urias's barn. Since moving to Grandma Mac's and then to her own place, she no longer kept it hidden.

She pulled out the note she'd written last night, in which she opened her heart completely to Shelton. She planned to give him the letter as a part of her wedding gift to him. She also removed a thin gold band she prayed would fit Shelton's ring finger.

She opened the door before he knocked.

"Good morning." His smile filled his handsome face.

"Have ye come to fetch me?" she said in her best Irish brogue.

Shelton chuckled. "Absolutely. All packed?"

"Trunk's there." She pointed to her left.

"What's this?" He nodded at the dining table. She'd set it with the fine linen tablecloth, matching napkins, and the horse-patterned china she had bought what seemed like ages ago.

He lifted a china plate. "This is very nice."

"It's one of the dowry items I purchased."

He put the dish back on the table. "I love it." He picked up the trunk and hefted in it the wagon. "I've made arrangements with the stable to house the buggy and horse for the few days we're on board the steamer."

"When's the next ship?"

"Not until tomorrow. We'll spend tonight in the hotel. I reserved a room and I've made arrangements at the tavern for dinner."

"You've thought of everything." She reached up to climb into the carriage.

"Allow me." Shelton swooped her into his arms and lifted her, brushing his lips lightly across hers.

"You're such a romantic."

He winked. "I can be."

"I have a surprise for you, but you'll have to wait," she teased, patting the gold ring that sat in her pocket.

Shelton made his way around the wagon and got in on the other side. "I think I'm going to enjoy our marriage." He snapped the reins.

"I hope so. Where are we going to live after we get back?"

"At your little log cabin. I figure we'll build our own home on that peninsula overlooking the Cumberland as soon as we have the funds."

All the way to Creelsboro they talked about their future,

the desire for children, and their hopes and dreams. At the church, Katherine sequestered herself in a small room to get ready for the ceremony.

A gentle knock on the door was followed by Parson Kincaid's wife poking her head in. "Can I help?"

"Please. I'm so nervous I can't get this headpiece in my hair."

The plump, middle-aged woman came into the room. "Your dress is lovely. Did you make it yourself?"

"Yes."

"Gracious, you are an excellent seamstress. No wonder Mr. Hastings can't keep your shirts in the store for long. Did you make this headpiece as well?"

"Yes." Katherine fought the instinct to nod as she allowed Mrs. Kincaid to adjust the headpiece. "I can't believe I'm so nervous."

The woman gave her a conspiratorial wink. "Mr. Greene has just about worn a hole in my husband's office floor."

Really? The information helped her relax.

Mrs. Kincaid placed the veil over Katherine's red hair. "You're beautiful," she gushed.

She glanced in the mirror. Her reflection did look beautiful. She felt beautiful, too, knowing Shelton loved her no matter what her past held. She felt covered in his love and in God's cleansing love. "Thank you."

"Come down the aisle when you hear the music, child."

"I will."

A few minutes later Katherine heard the music. She reached for the crystal doorknob and took in a deep breath. "Help me, Lord." A gentle peace washed over her. Confidently, she pulled the door open and walked to the aisle. Down at the front stood Shelton, dressed in his Sunday best with his black trousers, white shirt, and black dress coat and tails. His deep blue eyes sparkled and his smile brightened his whole face.

Katherine took a tentative step forward. It seemed to take an eternity to walk down that aisle, yet in a moment she was standing by his side. He reached out and held her hand. They turned and faced Parson Kincaid.

She repeated the words the parson asked her to say. She heard Shelton proclaim his love. But she didn't feel married until their lips met. Her arms slipped around the man she loved, cradling and holding him with all the passion and love she had. And in that moment, she found what she'd been looking for all her life. In her love for Shelton, in being one with him, she found the place of her own that she had always longed for.

Their kiss deepened. Parson Kincaid cleared his throat.

Shelton pulled back. "I love you, Katherine."

"I love you, too."

A Letter To Our Readers

Dear Reader:
In order that we might better contribute to your reading enjoyment, we would appreciate your taking a few minutes to respond to the following questions. We welcome your comments and read each form and letter we receive. When completed, please return to the following:

Fiction Editor
Heartsong Presents
PO Box 719
Uhrichsville, Ohio 44683

1. Did you enjoy reading *A Place of Her Own* by Lynn A. Coleman?
   ❑ Very much! I would like to see more books by this author!
   ❑ Moderately. I would have enjoyed it more if
   ____
   ____
   ____

2. Are you a member of **Heartsong Presents**? ❑ Yes ❑ No
   If no, where did you purchase this book? ______________
   ____

3. How would you rate, on a scale from 1 (poor) to 5 (superior), the cover design? ______________

4. On a scale from 1 (poor) to 10 (superior), please rate the following elements.

____ Heroine	____ Plot
____ Hero	____ Inspirational theme
____ Setting	____ Secondary characters

5. These characters were special because? ______________

____

____

6. How has this book inspired your life? ______________

____

____

7. What settings would you like to see covered in future **Heartsong Presents** books? ______________

____

____

8. What are some inspirational themes you would like to see treated in future books? ______________

____

____

9. Would you be interested in reading other **Heartsong Presents** titles? ❑ Yes ❑ No

10. Please check your age range:

❑ Under 18 ❑ 18-24
❑ 25-34 ❑ 35-45
❑ 46-55 ❑ Over 55

Name ______________________________________
Occupation __________________________________
Address ____________________________________
City, State, Zip ______________________________

BROTHERS
OF THE OUTLAW TRAIL

4 stories in 1

Four first-rate authors bring the outlaw Wilson brothers—Reuben, Caleb, Colt, and Benjamin—to life in this daring collection of stories set in the historic Wild West. As the tales unfold, the reader is in for a feast of adventure, romance, and the transforming grace of faith in God.

Historical, paperback, 352 pages, 5³⁄₁₆" x 8"

Please send me ____ copies of *Brothers of the Outlaw Trail.*
I am enclosing $6.97 for each.
(Please add $2.00 to cover postage and handling per order. OH add 7% tax.)
Send check or money order, no cash or C.O.D.s, please.

Name ____

Address ______________________________________

City, State, Zip _________________________________

To place a credit card order, call 1-740-922-7280.
Send to: Heartsong Presents Readers' Service, PO Box 721, Uhrichsville, OH 44683

Presents

__HP627 *He Loves Me, He Loves Me Not,* R. Druten
__HP628 *Silent Heart,* B. Youree
__HP631 *Second Chance,* T. V. Bateman
__HP632 *Road to Forgiveness,* C. Cox
__HP635 *Hogtied,* L. A. Coleman
__HP636 *Renegade Husband,* D. Mills
__HP639 *Love's Denial,* T. H. Murray
__HP640 *Taking a Chance,* K. E. Hake
__HP643 *Escape to Sanctuary,* M. J. Conner
__HP644 *Making Amends,* J. L. Barton
__HP647 *Remember Me,* K. Comeaux
__HP648 *Last Chance,* C. M. Hake
__HP651 *Against the Tide,* R. Druten
__HP652 *A Love So Tender,* T. V. Batman
__HP655 *The Way Home,* M. Chapman
__HP656 *Pirate's Prize,* L. N. Dooley
__HP659 *Bayou Beginnings,* K. M. Y'Barbo
__HP660 *Hearts Twice Met,* F. Chrisman
__HP663 *Journeys,* T. H. Murray
__HP664 *Chance Adventure,* K. E. Hake
__HP667 *Sagebrush Christmas,* B. L. Etchison
__HP668 *Duel Love,* B. Youree
__HP671 *Sooner or Later,* V. McDonough
__HP672 *Chance of a Lifetime,* K. E. Hake
__HP672 *Bayou Secrets,* K. M. Y'Barbo
__HP672 *Beside Still Waters,* T. V. Bateman
__HP679 *Rose Kelly,* J. Spaeth
__HP680 *Rebecca's Heart,* L. Harris
__HP683 *A Gentlemen's Kiss,* K. Comeaux
__HP684 *Copper Sunrise,* C. Cox
__HP687 *The Ruse,* T. H. Murray
__HP688 *A Handful of Flowers,* C. M. Hake
__HP691 *Bayou Dreams,* K. M. Y'Barbo
__HP692 *The Oregon Escort,* S. P. Davis
__HP695 *Into the Deep,* L. Bliss
__HP696 *Bridal Veil,* C. M. Hake
__HP699 *Bittersweet Remembrance,* G. Fields
__HP700 *Where the River Flows,* I. Brand
__HP703 *Moving the Mountain,* Y. Lehman
__HP704 *No Buttons or Beaux,* C. M. Hake
__HP707 *Mariah's Hope,* M. J. Conner
__HP708 *The Prisoner's Wife,* S. P. Davis
__HP711 *A Gentle Fragrance,* P. Griffin
__HP712 *Spoke of Love,* C. M. Hake
__HP715 *Vera's Turn for Love,* T. H. Murray
__HP716 *Spinning Out of Control,* V. McDonough
__HP719 *Weaving A Future,* S. P. Davis
__HP720 *Bridge Across The Sea,* P. Griffen
__HP723 *Adam's Bride,* L. Harris
__HP724 *A Daughter's Quest,* L. N. Dooley

Great Inspirational Romance at a Great Price!

Heartsong Presents books are inspirational romances in contemporary and historical settings, designed to give you an enjoyable, spirit-lifting reading experience. You can choose wonderfully written titles from some of today's best authors like Peggy Darty, Sally Laity, DiAnn Mills, Colleen L. Reece, Debra White Smith, and many others.

When ordering quantities less than twelve, above titles are $2.97 each. Not all titles may be available at time of order.

SEND TO: **Heartsong Presents** Reader's Service
P.O. Box 721, Uhrichsville, Ohio 44683

Please send me the items checked above. I am enclosing $ ______ (please add $2.00 to cover postage per order. OH add 7% tax. NJ add 6%). Send check or money order, no cash or C.O.D.s, please.

To place a credit card order, call 1-740-922-7280.

NAME ______________________________

ADDRESS ______________________________

CITY/STATE ______________________ ZIP ________

HPS 1-07